DELTA GREEN:
Through a Glass, Darkly

Dennis Detwiller

ARC DREAM PUBLISHING • 2012

DEDICATION

For Grandma, Uncle Lloyd and Uncle John.

A very special thanks to N.B. and Craig Tohill,
who went above and beyond
in the service of the group.

Delta Green: Through a Glass, Darkly © 2011 Dennis Detwiller. Cover illustration by Dennis Detwiller, © 2011. Published by arrangement with the Delta Green Partnership. The intellectual property known as Delta Green is ™ and © The Delta Green Partnership, who has licensed its use in this novel. Quotations from other sources are © by their respective authors. All rights reserved worldwide.

Published March 2012 by Arc Dream Publishing
12215 Highway 11, Chelsea, AL 35043, USA
www.arcdream.com
First paperback printing
ISBN 978-0-9832313-5-6 (paperback edition)

Printed in the United States of America

CONTENTS

Part One: Six Impossible Things Before Breakfast 5

    In the Fugue 6

    The Call 8

    Like a Deep Sea Diver 12

    Two Tickets, Please 19

    The Clipping Service 24

    Special Deliveries 28

    Something Like a Wind Tunnel 33

    Coffee and Coffins 35

    Busy, Busy 41

    Not Who . . . What 45

    This *X-Files* Shit 50

    Conduits 54

    Done and Done 62

    There Are Others 65

Part Two: Life In the Fire 71

    Unknowns 72

    The Alamo 77

    Friendlies 86

    Kill Them All 92

    Need to Know 96

    Reunion, Class of '69 102

    A Rendezvous 107

Feints Within Feints 117

Part Three: The Architect **123**

Old Friends 124

Hello, Goodbye 134

Deals 139

The Sound of Infinity 144

The Bare Bones of It 148

Safeguards 152

Stimulus/Response 163

Kept Men 170

Devil, Details 183

Target 188

Last Dance 191

Coordinate 202

The Last Trick 204

Do You Want to See? 207

The Edge of Infinity 210

Resolution 215

Acknowledgements **217**

Part One: Six Impossible Things Before Breakfast

"For now we see through a glass, darkly; but then face to face: Now I know in part; but then shall I know even also as I am known. And now abideth faith, hope, charity, these three; but the greatest of these is charity."

—I Corinthians ch. 13, v. 12–13

"If the doors of perception were cleansed everything would appear to man as it is, infinite."

—William Blake

In the Fugue

At the Focus.

It wasn't a dream.

He was watching himself from above, but not in some abstract sense. He saw himself from a height of a dozen meters or more, cowering amid low-standing ferns with his M-16 forgotten at his feet, dressed in ridiculously oversized fatigues stained with red mud. Others were there, but they were lost in their own terror. Somehow, though he knew them, he couldn't place them. They weren't what drew his attention. He was looking at something which split the night like a magnesium flare. His face—younger than he recalled—was agape, considering what his mind wouldn't bring into focus. He looked terrified, seconds from death.

But that was not the only self he saw. He also stood in a stark hospital room, older now, covering his face with a hand that clutched a pistol, trying to shield his eyes. The shift from the first scene to the second was as simple as tilting one's head. In one corner of his vision he saw the jungle, in the other the hospital room. They were seamlessly connected. That same light played across the room, engulfing it, obscuring what was in the bed. A low hum pulsed like a rocketing freight train on a collision course with his mind, shaking everything like it would tear the world to pieces.

Even as he looked away, there were more hims, more selves. Now he stood, older still, in a long, narrow, tall hallway hung with timber rafters, and the same light spilled over him. The door at the end of the unfinished hall was open and filled with light. The sound was worse, but also fascinating—beautiful and haunting, like a lullaby recalled only by biological memory; something from far too early in life to recall properly, but which hung over a lifetime like unconscious knowledge.

He turned away and found himself face-to-face with himself—terrified, lost, lit by the blue-white light. Then he was himself, his other self, facing the light. Fearing to look too closely into the light, he turned again. Then again, quicker, and again. Soon the room was spinning in lazy flips, as he leapt from self to self through time. Looping. Closing the loop. Faster.

The music built to a crescendo as he found he could no longer look away from the light. The jumps were so fast now that his vision of the light was a staccato blast of a dozen different wiggling frames per second. There were shapes there in the light. The sounds and the shapes formed patterns. The patterns were *everything*. When his eyes tracked each pattern and each sound, the world froze. Each mote of existence hung in the air like a lazy snowflake, apparent, clear, perfect. Still.

When he woke with a startled jump at a sound from the room, he considered his shaking hands, and then slowly strapped on his pistol. Someday, he was certain, he would need it.

The Call

Collateral paranormal event: Rutgers University, New Brunswick, New Jersey. 40.48 N/74.46 W latitude/longitude: Monday, January 22, 2001, 4:37 A.M. EST.

WHEN THE CALL CAME, Brady Commons was lit in dark, pastel tones. The quad was empty, lit here and there by arc lamps and an amber sky that was gaining a clear, still light—the type that would cook off the fog before dawn ever came. It was not morning, at least not yet; there were hours left until the students would rise and go about their business.

Now was the time of empty hallways. Of flickering fluorescent lamps and the soothing hum and click of unattended soda machines, of the pulsing rhythms of the boiler in the bowels of the building, chugging away like a buried beast. It was a time rich with the energy that moves in the air when no one is around, the sensation of events perched on the edge of occurring, the feeling of tension gathering silently in the air like a storm—the force of a spring compressing in a mechanism ready to trigger a countdown.

When the phone rang at four thirty-seven in the morning in room 3A, it rang only once. Usually a phone at this time of the morning would ring on and on while someone stumbled through the dark to find out who had died. It was always bad news at a time like this. In a way, this call was no different. The news was bad, though the caller and man who answered would not realize how bad until much, much later.

The person next to this particular phone had been sleeping on the floor in front of the television set, with a single meaty arm on the shelf next to the receiver and his head propped up on the edge of the couch, since two thirty-four. His jerky rise to consciousness, all elbows and knees, knocked the receiver off the hook before it could ring again. Lost in a sea of fast-food cartons and half-eaten Doritos bags, the man looked like a casualty in the war on obesity. His Rutgers T-shirt, stained with various sauces and beverages, had not seen detergent in more than a year.

He rose to a soupy semi-consciousness and jiggled as he coughed and rubbed his pimpled face. The receiver chattered away on the table; a disembodied chipmunk-like voice poured from the earpiece.

The man tried to press down his hair, stuck up in loose brown cowlicks held together by spit, sleep and drying food, but it immediately returned to its former state of chaos.

The fat man fumbled for the receiver on the table, which slipped away from his grasp like a fish and dropped to the nappy burgundy rug at his hip. Then, somehow he managed to scoop the ugly handset up in both hands. He didn't open his eyes. The room was dark except for the television flashing an endless, snow-like static. He connected the right end of the phone to his right ear. The chipmunk voice was still babbling away on the other end.

"Garrity . . . hmch . . . Garrity here," the fat man said, finally.

The voice on the line, which had been talking the whole time, paused for a second to emit a stuttering sound of disgust, then continued in a higher, more urgent tone.

"Shut up! Garrity, shut up. Bob Lumsden broke Violet 5. He's gone. I don't know what happened. He's gone. Did I say that? It worked. The program worked. I'll be fucked if it didn't work. It worked. He's gone. It worked. What did we do, Garrity? What the fuck—Garrity? Are you there?"

"Garrity here," the fat man replied, nonplussed. Nothing had registered. It was all gibberish. The only thing he recognized was his name.

"What the fuck do we do?"

"I come down and see what happened," he said.

"What?"

"I–COME–DOWN–TO–THE–LAB!" Garrity shouted, his voice tired and hoarse.

"But did you hear me? He's fuckin' gone! Lumsden's gone!"

"Where'd he go?" Garrity yawned.

"He disappeared in front of me and Loew, in the machine. Loew's curled in the corner like some sort of—I don't know. Shit."

Garrity stood up in the dark, pulling the phone's base off the table. It hit the ground and made an angry ringing noise that slowly echoed into silence.

"Was it on? Was the Glass active?"

"WEREN'T YOU FUCKING LISTENING HE BROKE VIOLET 5!"

"Keep it down, Mitchell, no one's ever broken Violet 5," Garrity whispered.

"My program worked. We sidestepped the error. It worked."

"Worked," Garrity echoed, his voice empty of all emotion.

Something dark and empty settled in Garrity's stomach. It took more than a minute to realize that for all his breakthroughs and inventions and knowledge, an unreasoning fear held him frozen. Waiting for more information. Three miles away on the other end of the line, Mitchell breathed into the phone but remained silent. Beneath the breathing, Garrity heard a static-filled chorus of voices, mistransmissions that bled through on the line.

Garrity hung up the phone and stared at the static-covered television. After a moment, he clicked it off with the remote.

"Violet 5," he said to no one at all. And then began to dress in the dark, retrieving his shoes and pants from a pile of clothing under the table that held the television.

He didn't know what to feel, but one thing seemed obvious: Either he had lost his mind or Mitchell had. *(Or maybe,* his analytical mind chimed in, *they had lost their minds simultaneously.)* Other options were there, of course. Other possibilities—but they were difficult to think about.

People did not disappear. Loew, ever stable, did not break down. There were general rules to the universe. Doritos made you fat. The television played static after four if you didn't have cable. There were stars in the sky.

But he had read so much to the contrary, so much that he had put into the construction of the Looking-Glass.

The world doesn't really make sense, does it, he thought. *It never has, and you've always known it, everyone knows it. Some choose to ignore that feeling, some—*

With effort he pushed the thoughts away. He had been entertaining them, the same thoughts that led to his career and construction of the Looking-Glass, since before he could remember. They had always been there.

Please let me believe that Lumsden's just playing a joke, he silently pleaded as he pulled out of the parking lot in his clunky Daihatsu.

But he didn't believe. They weren't friends and he knew it. They were geniuses who tolerated each other so they would have someone to prove wrong and to get done what needed to get done. What Mitchell said happened, had happened. He knew it. But what if it was all a mistake?

Something wouldn't let him find comfort in that simple thought.

"Please God, let me believe in something," he said aloud in the car. His voice sounded so hollow, so tinny in the stutter of the sewing-machine engine that he found no solace in the muttered prayer.

The first and last sincere prayer he would utter in his adult life.

Like a Deep Sea Diver

Class Two paranormal event: Tesoro Station, Snohomish County, Washington. 47.96 N/122.00 W latitude/longitude. Approximately 2,378 miles from New Brunswick: Friday, January 26, 2001, 2:37 A.M. PST.

TIM MORIARITY SAT IN the Tesoro gas station behind three inches of bulletproof glass and watched the lights on the highway, feeling something move through him like defeat. With it, the same old disbelief and nostalgia rose up in his throat. How had he arrived here? What had he done to deserve this job? This life? It all seemed unfair. He could not locate any event on which he could pin the blame. Any particular event would do—some memory under which he could sweep the crap away, something he could label: THE MISTAKE. He wasn't picky, really.

Anything.

His whole life seemed like one prolonged mistake. Maybe that's why he couldn't localize it.

His life was scattered across the western half of the United States like the contents of a ransacked apartment, from its starting point in Philadelphia to its apparent finish line: a booth on the outskirts of Seattle at two A.M., enduring the ass end of a swing shift like the last months of a twenty-year prison sentence.

His life was composed of equal parts distrust, hate and boredom. All the necessary components for a Jerry Springer show (hell, a half a dozen of them) were there. Two ex-wives (only one of whom knew where he was), four children he never saw, several abandoned pets, apartments full of crap (along with months' and months' worth of overdue rent at each) and three cars (one of them new). Now all of these things, people and possessions were gone, each and every one. All sucked somewhere into the endless expanse of the country. He had no phone numbers, no addresses, no paperwork, no keys and no attachments. He couldn't locate any of them now and he no longer tried. He had left, after all. Who would want to hear from him?

Hell, he didn't even want to hear from himself. Isn't that what this boredom was all about?

He probably couldn't even pick his kids out of a police lineup—which is where they would turn up anyway in a couple of years, after the way he had destroyed them. Didn't he know how it felt? Hadn't his dad done the same thing to him?

Once this life had seemed ideal. No connection to the past, an endless open future. But now, as he hit the end of the country, it seemed he had also hit the end of what passed for a life. Seattle was it—as far west as he could go without swimming, as his dad used to say. It pulled him in. He had a good apartment, a shitty job, a terrible boss and no real friends. All in all, a normal life, a normal existence. But why then did he—

There was a knock at the window.

Moriarity jumped, and a lancing pain shot across his lap as coffee spilled over his legs. A steaming trail had traced a river across the sports pages of the *Seattle Times* and off the counter. Scooping up the wet newspaper, Moriarity dammed the coffee off and wiped it back into a messy pile of wet newsprint until only a few streaks remained on the counter. He rapidly righted the cup and stared out the glass window, his face set in an exasperated frown.

Though he could not be sure, for a moment Moriarity could swear that the figure beyond the glass looked somehow blurred. Shaky, as if viewed from underwater, like it was rising out of the air itself, solid but indistinct. Just as suddenly it was all right. He was looking at a rather plain man in a beaten denim jacket and jogging pants. The stranger's hair was neatly combed, his face clean and pleasant.

The stranger's long and thin face split in a self-deprecating smile, embarrassed and a little bit sad.

Moriarity depressed the speaker button.

"What can I do for you?"

He was expecting a request for change (Tesoro's prices were not very competitive at the moment) or maybe even a small amount of gas from Pump 1 (super unleaded, the cheapest). Instead the man squinted, fixing him with a confused stare, the look of someone trying to good-naturedly puzzle something out. Moriarity noticed for the first time that there were no cars at either of the pump islands. Moriarity unlocked the cash drawer and looked down at the pistol in it.

"Tim?" the man asked. He had a shy, retiring voice that was nonetheless full of some kind of good humor. For no reason he could place, Tim Moriarity thought of sneakers. The image rose clearly in his mind, but it meant nothing.

"Yeah?" Moriarity barked back through the speaker, voice distant and full of suspicion.

"Tim Moriarity?" the man reiterated.

"Yeah?"

"It's me. Bob Lumsden. We went to high school together."

"Bob . . . " Tim said, considering. It had been a long time, after all—ten years—something like that. Thomas Jefferson High School, Philadelphia, Pennsylvania, class of '89.

"Lumsden? Bob . . . I remember you! We had gym together!" Moriarity shouted, his voice full of the first bit of real pleasure he had felt in many months. Bobby Lumsden had been a . . . well, he had been a wimp. Someone Tim and the football crew picked on pretty heavily; but that was a long time ago. It seemed like a lifetime ago, now, like it had happened to another person.

Hopefully Lumsden felt the same.

"That's me." Lumsden modestly smiled.

"So . . . " Moriarity began, and then found himself at a loss. So what? What did he have to say to Lumsden? Not much. Still, here he was, a connection to his past, even if it was technically speaking a bad one. Lumsden was all he knew in Seattle that could lay claim to his own existence before his arrival. Lumsden was the only proof in this town that Moriarity had led a life before arriving at this gas station. Suddenly it seemed terribly important to talk to Bob Lumsden, but the words wouldn't come.

"What have you been doing with yourself?" Lumsden inserted, filling the awkward silence that had spun out.

"Oh, nothing much," Tim replied, smiling as if to say, You know, the same old stuff. He shrugged.

"Still raping teenage girls?" Lumsden asked, in the same tone one would use to ask a stranger for the time.

Silence spun out again.

"I think you better get out of here, shithead," Moriarity finally hissed through clenched teeth.

Lumsden looked at Moriarity and shook his head sadly.

"I'm going to tell you something, Tim. Something not many people ever get to know. You see, it gets hard to think clearly when the time comes. It gets hard to think, when you go through. But I learned the trick. I went through and I came back, and you know what I learned?"

Moriarity said nothing; instead he picked up the receiver of the telephone and began dialing 911. He stopped after two digits and glanced down at the half-open cash drawer. Lumsden had obviously waltzed off the deep end a long time ago. But what could he do? Call the police and open a whole new can of worms? What the hell was the girl's name anyway? Sarah . . . something. Beer, cigarettes and some pointless Eighties tune rose up at the thought of her name.

Pinning her down and covering her mouth. To him, it would never be rape.

Tim Moriarity was drawn back to the present by a tapping at the window. The madman stared at him mildly through the Plexiglas. The expression on Lumsden's face was one of an exuberant teacher, one who was not content to let anybody slip by without learning their lesson.

"It's this I want to tell you, Tim, and listen carefully, because I won't repeat it. 'Whatever you're thinking about in the last second of your life is what you think about forever.' I think, Tim—well, hell—I know you'll be thinking of Sarah."

That was it. Something inside him white hot and deadly leapt up and took control. Moriarity retrieved the snub-nose revolver from the cash drawer and fumbled to unlock the booth, feeling like both actions were performed in slow motion. He stepped into the wet Seattle night waving the pistol around like a frightened idiot, trying to prove his resolve through action. Moriarity attempted to gain a foothold on the situation. Events were rapidly spiraling out of control. Hadn't he been quietly reading the sports pages and drinking coffee just a minute ago?

He said, "You just shut up, Lumsden, you don't know anything. I could shoot you right now and tell the cops you threatened to rob me." But his voice sounded scared and weak. Still, something was growing in him. Hate? Disbelief? He didn't know. It was big and it felt strong, but jittery and out of control at the same time.

Moriarity grinned unsteadily, his equilibrium somewhat restored. The natural balance of things had gone askew with Lumsden's accusation, but it seemed corrected now that the shithead was on the business end of the pistol.

"What would you shoot me with, Tim?" Lumsden idiotically asked. Was he blind as well as crazy? What the—

Moriarity's eyes bulged.

The gun was gone from his hand. His fingers were still poised as if they held a gun. His calloused index finger was still curled around a non-existent trigger. His arm was foolishly raised from his hip and pointed at Lumsden, as if it could actually do something other than point. His hand felt warm and tingly. Strange, but not hot. In the January air a thin, wispy cloud of steam seemed to flow for a moment from the cup of his palm.

"Oops," Lumsden laughed.

"What the fuck—" Moriarity whispered, the first hint of fear creeping into his voice.

"It's like this, Tim. It's like I can see all this happening, it's like I can see everything happening. On the other side . . . this whole world is so clear. But I can't affect it from there. But when I come back through, well, that's a different story. I can't see half as well, but I can do things. I can do things." Lumsden clapped his hands, pleased with himself. There was a sudden metallic clatter from the right. Moriarity jumped at the sound and spun. Over at the nearest pump he saw the snub-nose .38 lying on the cement, lit in the harsh lamps. It was more than twenty feet on the other side of Lumsden.

It was the gun Moriarty had been holding a second before. But there was no way that could have just happened. A thin wisp of steam curled up from the grip of the pistol and was lost in the lights.

"What the hell—" Moriarity choked out. He began to back-pedal toward the booth's door.

"Good trick, huh?" Lumsden offered, smiling a sly smile.

"How did you do that?" Moriarity wheezed. The world seemed to swim before his eyes. It faded for a moment into a grey haze, only to return to crystal clarity, lit by colors that seemed to burn his eyes. It hit him like a slap, the reality of the situation. He realized Lumsden had been speaking the whole time, but he caught only the last half of the speech over the pounding of his heart.

"—coming back isn't that pleasant. Like I said, most, well, almost all people can't do it, but I can. It's like I'm a deep-sea diver. I put on my gear and come on through. This body, these forms, they're nothing more than a container for something so big you can't even begin to get it. They're like fuckin' Tinkertoys, fuckin' Legos. But I came back to set some things straight. To fulfill some promises. This one's for Sarah."

When Moriarity turned to step back into the safety of the booth he froze. His jaw dropped. His eyes, which had seemed up to be open as wide as possible, bulged wider in their sockets. A single clear line of drool spilled from his lips and struck his collar.

The door that had once been behind him—the door he had just come through—was gone, replaced by an expanse of tile with steam pouring from the grout. It was as if the door itself was a wound that the building had naturally scabbed over and healed. The booth appeared to have no entrance at all, just the Plexiglas window.

Moriarity placed his palms against the smooth, slightly wet surface of the wall and began to cry. It was real.

"Not fair. It's not fair," he wept.

"No, Tim. For the first time in a really long time, things are going to be fair."

Moriarity turned to look at Lumsden as the man's brow furrowed. Something gathered in the air, humming like an electrical charge. Like a train approaching a station at top speed.

"For my next trick . . ."

The screaming went on for a long time.

Two Tickets, Please

Initial conspiracy cell contact: JFK International Airport, Queens, New York. 40.64 N/73.79 W latitude/longitude. Approximately 2,399 miles from Snohomish County: Tuesday, January 30, 2001, 3:41 P.M. EST.

SUNBURNED AND SQUINTY, CURTIS McRay stepped into the worst winter New York had experienced in thirty years. During his first vacation in five years (alone, thank you very much), McRay had sat on the beach at St. Thomas like some sort of plant, absorbing sunlight and slowly changing colors—and drinking. Much to his chagrin, he found he had forgotten how to have fun. He knew only how to unwind. Drinking every night, baking every day, sleeping in and eating out. Now he was back from fantasyland, looking red and out of place among the snow-bleached natives of the Big Apple. At least he still had about a week before he was due back at the Buffalo office. Time enough to wind himself back up to the breakneck speed of federal law enforcement.

It had to be ten below with the wind chill, but JFK warmed his heart. People were being ticketed, yelling at ticketers, double-parking, unloading in the no-unloading zone, and entering unmarked, unlicensed cabs. New Yorkers always reminded him of the endless chattering of the monkey cage at the Bronx zoo. Little furry people hitting each other and flinging dung at innocent passersby. Without tails, of course, but basically the same. This sensation did not make McRay feel as one might think. It wasn't a bad sensation. It was a warm, cheery feeling: *I'm back in that cage*—thank God. He looked goofy, standing there, a gawky man in a light coat amid a sea of freezing pedestrians. His weasel-like face, topped with shaggy brown hair, was broken in a grin even though his bulky Buddy Holly glasses were coated with fog. He stood for a while in the nasty weather and breathed it all in: New York.

"Home," he contentedly sighed. A Pakistani cab driver (apparently licensed) threw a chunk of ice from his windshield at a black cab driver (obviously unlicensed) who had stolen his fare by knocking ten dollars off the outrageous price for a ride to Queens—which, needless to say, they were already in. All this took place a few feet from a bored transit cop who considered an interesting piece of snot he had removed from his nose with a meaty pinky. Nothing came of the ice attack. The projectile bounced off the black driver's windshield as he laughed and pulled away with two terrified elderly passengers in the back seat. They looked like they had just leapt to life from the pages of Our Town.

McRay lifted his luggage (he was slipping—you never let your luggage out of your hand at JFK, much less out of sight) and felt the wind cut into his sunburned face like razors. Someone shuffled up uncomfortably close behind him from the Delta terminal. McRay felt a single cold finger settle at the base of his skull. He spun comically.

"Bang," Poe said, face empty of emotion.

Donald Poe lowered his left hand, poised in the shape of an imaginary gun, to an imaginary holster at the hip of his battered camouflage jacket. His heart jumping wildly, McRay began to laugh and let his hand drop away from his shoulder rig. There were some perks to being a fed; carrying a pistol on a plane ride was one of them. It had long since gotten to the point where he almost felt naked without it.

"I could have shot you, you old dumb hick," McRay laughed in a plume of steam, and then clapped the huge man on the back. Poe stared back impassively, but a hint of a smile bled through. The hick was indeed getting old, but he looked solid enough to play professional football. Age had not yet consumed his natural bulk or turned it to fat, something that seemed to occur after retirement in most men. That was a good thing; there weren't too many in the group like Poe.

You didn't retire from the group. No one retired from the group. Maybe that's what keeps Poe going, McRay thought.

To McRay, Poe would always look like some sort of aging professional wrestler. Dressed in camo, boots and a John Deere cap, the squarely-built giant looked exactly like the type of gun-toting militiaman that had the FBI all in a twist. But he had humped it in the jungles for his country in the Sixties and had spent his fair share of time in "the dark" after his return. Hell, they both had had seen their share of some seriously spooky shit. McRay was only a little more than half the bigger man's age but the two had spent some of the most harrowing moments of their lives together.

Poe emptying the contents of a Mossberg shotgun into a glowing man. The memory swam up in McRay's mind like an untethered balloon drifting by in the dark, and he tried to push it away. *Ronald Valiant was the man's name,* the quiet voice in his head intoned. *Valiant was like Superman because there were things that gave him power, things that clicked like bugs, like giant Maine lobsters, like—*

Enough. It was hard to think about the specifics. It was the little things that got to you.

They had paid their debts, or so he liked to imagine. But it was never over, once you were in; it was never over until you were over. It had taken McRay nine years to learn that. Poe had taught him by example. Donald A. Poe—"Charlie" to those within the conspiracy—was the model agent of Delta Green.

"I don't see how you could have shot me," Poe replied quietly, in a gravelly voice. The burn scar on his cheek rippled in time with the words. "I shot you first." Someone laid on a horn so hard and so long McRay was sure some mechanical failure had occurred. Poe didn't even flinch.

"Let me guess: bad news?" McRay sighed. Suddenly he was glad he had cashed in a month of vacation time. He had planned on visiting New York City for two weeks before drifting back into the Buffalo FBI office. Now, it seemed, he would be on an op instead.

"Nice tan. Yeah, I got the call yesterday. Came through Benton. Two tickets to the Opera. We're on a plane in," Poe glanced at his huge silver watch, "twenty-two minutes."

"So what's the deal? Missing person? Creature feature?"

Poe grabbed one of McRay's bags—the big one, like it was filled with tissue paper—and walked back into the Delta terminal. McRay followed. Poe said something but it was lost in the mechanical slam of the doors.

"What?"

"I said, 'Found person.'"

"I didn't get you."

"I said, 'Found person.'"

"What?" McRay stopped in the terminal and people fluttered by, maneuvering around him with contempt in their eyes. Poe stopped and turned to look at him, his voice even and quiet. Around them the world went on and on, secure in its own importance.

"Michael Lumsden, age nine, was found asleep in his parents' house six days ago in suburban Pennsylvania, outside of Philadelphia. The boy had been missing for more than ten years."

"Ten years? Age nine?"

"Yeah," Poe muttered back, his voice dropping. Something like fear was in his tone, but something else was there as well, something like certainty. McRay watched closely to see if he was setting up one of his rarely seen jokes, but his icy blue eyes stared back empty of any humor.

"So?" McRay laughed nervously. "I guess, good for the Lumsdens, right? Who took him?"

"Cancer took him. Michael Lumsden died at Philadelphia Children's Hospital on October 5, 1990, of leukemia. He was two days short of his tenth birthday."

It didn't matter how long you had the job, the ops still had a way of punching through anything you placed in their way. Work, life, the world meant nothing in the face of what McRay and Poe confronted. You never got used to it. It never became routine. Maybe that was its draw. Why so many had signed on and so many had died.

And there were always more bodies coming down the chute.

Poe turned and continued to check in. McRay stood for a moment, watching the man disappear into the crowd.

"That's all I fucking need," he said to himself. "Another night at the fucking Opera." He followed Poe.

The Clipping Service

Official notice of Class One paranormal event: The "Country Club," outside Mount Weather, Virginia. 38.98 N/76.50 W latitude/longitude. Approximately 241 miles from Queens: Monday, February 5, 2001, 1:12 P.M. EST.

THE THIN MAN APPROACHED the security checkpoint and presented his credentials. A guard considered him with the piercing stare of a sentry on the edge of enemy territory.

The thin man stood stock still with his hands on the desk as the guard slipped the badge through the machine. A green light lit on the device.

"Hand on the scanner, please, sir," the guard ordered. The thin man knew that below the plain-looking desk a submachine gun was pointed directly at his crotch. If the light did not come on, if the chime on the palm scanner did not sound a "Ding!", the thin man would not be long for this world. He would be cut in half by automatic fire in the middle of all this splendor and perfect architecture. If his bona fides were not up to snuff, he was dead. Even if there were some kind of computer glitch, he would be an ex-member of MAJESTIC and of the human race, in that order.

The warmth of the light from the scanner ran up and then down his palm, followed rapidly by a loud "DING!" Something loosened in his chest.

Not today, he thought.

"You are free to pass, sir," the guard said, and his voice held a distant note of regret.

Fucking black-ops DELTA psychos, Martin Glenn thought. A buzzer sounded as the guard unlocked the tan double doors, and he passed through.

Perched precariously on the edge of an immense desk covered

in papers, Charles Bostick glanced up as Glenn entered.

"Marty, what's up?"

"I just got this from the national clipping service. It looks like another Class One event, something for Yrjo and the boys. Ross is going to want a piece of it, too. We're lucky the facility is in such a shambles. How long until OUTLOOK is back up and running?"

"A month, maybe more. Shit," Bostick cursed and stood up. His soda-stained shirt hung from an undone belt and his hair stood up in sleep-sculpted strands. They had just finished erasing the "deaths" of twenty-three men who went missing from Fort Benning in late June under circumstances best not considered. Thirteen men had spent three months rewriting files, changing dates, moving reports, misplacing and destroying and doctoring personnel records all the way down to individual gas receipts and photographs. With the illusion complete, they hoped, each family would believe that only their loved one had simply gone AWOL.

If not, other resources would be tapped. It was a complex shuck and jive. MAJESTIC was good at it because it had done it so many times. It was their most basic play: Cover it up and deny it all. It was best not to think of how much there was to eliminate. The jobs just kept coming, each more complex than the last. Walking corpses, alien parasites and spaceships.

MAJESTIC was lucky to have a master at the wheel of their disinformation machine. That master was Charlie Bostick.

Martin Glenn handed the sheet over. In the past few years Bostick had perfected the classic technique, honing what had been a blunt tool to a wicked razor's edge. Before his arrival, going back to 1947, the group would muscle in, throw some weight around and crush anyone who failed to toe the government line—UFOs did not exist, and neither did anything smacking of UFOs. It was expensive. It was a lot of work and it led to its own set of problems.

Bostick had simply pointed out the obvious: What the MAJESTIC study group dealt with, for the most part, sounded just plain ridiculous to anyone outside the group. With his new program there were no more heavy-handed black ops, outside of closing off a few persistent loose ends. Instead the group applied a little disinformation here, some misleading data there, a few small character assassinations, and voilà, the mystery—the darkness that the group covered up—vanished like a media magic trick. For the most part there was no need for cordons and containment and guns. People didn't believe in aliens and spaceships and monsters from other dimensions. Their disbelief was the lever on which human thought could be moved.

Bostick manned that lever.

Bostick knew people better than they knew themselves. He was a walking encyclopedia of fringe lore and factual weirdness, a cross-referencing media machine.

But he didn't look like a genius. He looked like a formerly happy man who has just now found out some terrible truth about life.

FINGERPRINTS CONFIRM MYSTERIOUS YOUTH IS MICHAEL LUMSDEN, the tabloid headlines shouted. NINE-YEAR-OLD RETURNS FROM THE GRAVE. FAMILY WITHHOLDS COMMENT. Bostick scanned the stories rapidly.

"Sweet Jesus," Bostick muttered, mostly to himself. "How the fuck are we going to cover this up? This shit's like media heroin. They will report on this one story until they die. Even I couldn't come up with shit this sweet. . . ."

Martin Glenn could hear Justin Kroft's answer already, and now he and Bostick said it together in unison—the standard, pat answer they always were given by the steering committee.

"Just cover it up," they both said glumly. Then they sat down and got on with it.

A look of confusion spilled over Bostick's sallow face—then the look of something clicking into place. Hard. He jumped up and snatched a file from the edge of his desk and rapidly leafed through the pages. He settled on something, a name, circled it and then checked another in a newspaper article.

"Oh shit, they match, I think. What does that mean?" Bostick said in a strangled voice, biting his thumbnail, "I—I got a feeling about this one...."

"What do we do now?" Glenn asked.

"We go to Philadelphia and find some yearbooks from Thomas Jefferson High School for 1989. Then we get Kroft on the horn."

Special Deliveries

Collateral paranormal event: The Sinclair Building, Cincinnati, Ohio. 39.11 N/84.53 W latitude/longitude. Approximately 431 miles from Mount Weather, Virginia: Sunday, January 28, 2001, 5:42 P.M. EST.

SARAH WATSON SAT ON the edge of the sofa with a beer in one hand and a newspaper in the other, considering the mute television from time to time with fleeting glances. She looked like a woman who had once been a pretty teenager but who had been subjected to years of rigorous and systematic psychological torture. It was called her job. Waitressing was its own private circle of hell, whose subtle tortures could never be understood by the uninitiated.

A story about a woman who killed her two children with poison (Liquid Plum-R) led the headlines of the *Cincinnati Journal*, while on the television a group of foreign-looking men dressed in weird camouflage outfits smiled with rotted yellow teeth at the camera. "OUTSIDE GROZNY," the caption read on the screen.

Whatever.

Sarah stretched out, feeling a decent buzz from the beer, reading with a kind of disconnected shock the story of the murdering mom. How someone could do something like that, she had no idea. Things like that happened in the world all the time, she was certain. She had first-hand experience with the horrors of real life. She knew from an early age that things did not turn out right, knew it even before her entry to the work-a-day world. It took a sharp eye and a distrustful nature to get by without a scratch. And some scratches were deep.

Sarah had tried to pass this on to her kid—the bitter facts. But through some sick practical joke of nature, Naomi was identical to Sarah at that age: fourteen. Fantastic fourteen, fearless fourteen. That was the last time Sarah could remember feeling safe, feeling truly without fear. Sarah at fourteen in the far-off year nineteen hundred and eighty-five. Crazed, without any rules, alive.

It had all come screeching to a halt, of course. Stopped in its tracks. One drunken night, her fearless, normal life was derailed. Oh, how she wanted to keep that feeling from Naomi. She would do anything to keep it from the kid. To keep the kid away from the shitty world that she had come to know so well. But nothing Sarah had to say was any good. The kid did what the kid wanted, and that was that.

What were you going to do? It was a crappy rendition of the same old story.

Sarah finished the beer in one long tug and stood up. She stretched and switched the TV off with the old, tape-covered remote and glanced towards the kitchen.

The shadow of a man was clearly visible on the tile floor.

Her breath caught in her throat and her heart skipped a beat before it started hammering away at four times its normal speed. For no good reason, she looked down at the remote in her hand. Then she had the presence of mind to freeze.

Before she could think of what to do next, the deep grey shadow seemed to lighten and then to *fade*. Not to move or vanish, but *diminish*. The other shadows in the room from the table and the chairs did not change. The man's shadow evaporated from the surface of the tile in seconds, vanished from the off-white glaze like a wisp of smoke. A tiny sound slipped from her mouth, something like a moan.

A sound came from the kitchen just as the last vestiges of the shadow vanished: a soft thud, the sound of paper hitting a hard surface. She had to cover her mouth to keep in the scream. It died in her throat, and all that came through her clenched fingers was a high hissing sound.

After a time, as she always did, Sarah began to doubt herself.

She had made some mistake. She had failed to understand what she was seeing. Anyway, what did she think she had seen? A ghost? No other sounds came from the kitchen. No noise from the notoriously creaky floor. Could someone still be in the tiny room without her knowing it? How the hell would someone get in there without her hearing? Without her seeing?

Sarah darted into the kitchen before she knew exactly what she planned to do.

A damp newspaper lay on the battered Formica table. It had not been there before. She was sure of that; she had just cleaned. The two windows in the kitchen—the only other entrances—were shut and bolted. No broken glass. No jimmied locks. Just a newspaper and the buzzing clock on the wall. Water gathered beneath the paper on the table in dribs and drabs.

Sarah walked slowly to the newspaper and noticed first that it was not one of the local papers.

SEATTLE POST-INTELLIGENCER, the banner read.

Seconds spun by before she placed the remote on the table next to it.

Finally, she lifted the newspaper and unfolded it so she could see the front page. Its pages were damp and sticky and she noticed fingerprints in the black ink of the cover, prints too long and thin to be her own.

GAS CLERK DIES UNDER STRANGE CIRCUMSTANCES, the headline read. The article had been circled in thick, black pencil. Sarah scanned it. She felt her heart catch in her chest when she read the name of the victim.

She sat down roughly, feeling like something in her was descending at a maddening speed, like the house was plummeting in freefall with everything in it. She read the article again and felt tears well up in her eyes. The tears just kept on coming, until it was a torrent, and she leapt up to grab some paper towels to get herself under control before the kid got back. God knew what she would think about her rough-and-tumble mom weeping away in the kitchen like a girl.

Sarah laughed at that, and placed the newspaper down on the table, wiping her bright red nose with a paper towel. That was when she noticed the paper bag beneath the table, behind the chairs.

On the paper bag—a grocery bag, tan, and also slightly wet—were printed the nonsensical words BON MARCHÉ. They meant nothing to her. She squatted down to pull the sack out from under the table and it slid heavily across the tile. Its sides bulged and crackled as it moved. When the opening of the bag slid into view, Sarah dropped backwards roughly onto her ass and let out a grunt, tipping the bag over, a look of utter shock on her puffy red face.

A wave of money—twenties, tens and fives—spilled out of the bag all over the tile floor, piling in drifts against her outstretched legs, more than she could count. A ton of bills. Thousands, no, tens of thousands of dollars' worth of bills.

A fortune.

Sarah lifted the only thing that stood out from the pile of crisp new bills, a single damp sheet of paper. It was an old college-ruled sheet of loose-leaf with three holes punched in it. Its edges were yellow with age.

FOR THE KID, the note stated in a sharp—almost familiar—print. It had been written with a marker and the ink was fresh. The sharp smell of it was still in the air.

Sarah began to laugh. It was a crazy sound, too high and too long to be a natural reaction. She stuffed bills back into the large shopping bag, laughing and crying at intervals while she scooped up the treasure. Soon Naomi would be home. Sarah was sure of one thing: The kid would know nothing about any of this.

No one could know anything about this.

Except maybe some bill collectors.

What the fuck was going on here? The dull monotony of her life had been shattered into a million pieces by a shadow, and what had been a mediocre day had suddenly become the greatest and most emotional day of her young life.

Life.

Something Like a Wind Tunnel

From the Seattle Post-Intelligencer, *Sunday, January 28, 2001.*

Gas Clerk Dies Under Strange Circumstances
Police Withhold Official Comment on 'Bizarre' Scene

By Martin Frendal (AP)

SNOHOMISH—The remains of Timothy P. Moriarity, 29, of Seattle, were discovered by Snohomish County deputies Friday morning in a culvert behind the Tesoro gas station at Dubuque Road and 171st Avenue Southeast.

The Snohomish County Sheriff's Office had no official comment, but one investigator said that the case was "bizarre."

"I've never seen anything like that body before in my life," said a detective at the scene.

When asked if foul play was suspected in Moriarity's death, Sheriff Todd Welton would only say that the matter was being examined at length and that he would make a further statement after the autopsy was completed by the Snohomish County medical examiner. The autopsy is scheduled for Wednesday.

Moriarity's mutilated body was found in a small drainage ditch behind the Tesoro gas station, where he was working at the time of his death. The exact cause of death is unknown. Robbery has been ruled out, though sources at the Snohomish County Sheriff's Office would not say why.

"There are a lot of unexplained things in this case," one source said, requesting anonymity. "Someone did this to him. He sure as hell didn't do it to himself. And some other bizarre evidence is on hand."

The site has been closed to the press.

When asked whether a weapon was used to kill Timothy Moriarity, the source said, "I don't know what could do what I saw. Something like a wind tunnel filled with sand, maybe."

Snohomish County authorities confirmed that Timothy Moriarity's parents, Scott and Helena Moriarity of Philadelphia, Pennsylvania, have been notified and are expected to arrive at Seattle within the week. Funeral arrangements will be announced later this week.

—See **'Mysterious Death,' A9**

Coffee and Coffins

Initial conspiracy Friendly contact: 1651 West Garrison Street, Philadelphia, Pennsylvania. 39.93 N/75.18 W latitude/longitude. Approximately 501 miles from Cincinnati: Tuesday, January 30, 2001, 8:19 P.M. EST.

"So, what's the story with the Friendly?" McRay asked through a mouth full of Fritos as Poe swerved the rent-a-car down unfamiliar streets.

Philadelphia was cold and uninviting. There wasn't snow on the ground, but every windshield they passed was a sheet of ice and no one walked the streets. Houses stared at them with flat, brightly lit windows, but shades were drawn and doors were shut.

"Can't you see I'm driving? Eat your food," Poe said and switched on the radio. He looked ridiculous, a huge man behind the wheel of a cramped car, even more so when he carefully adjusted the tuner on the radio. A Beatles-esque song called "Wonderwall" was in its last strains on the local rock station.

"Yeah, and I'm eating. So what's the dirt on the Friendly?"

"Edwards?" Poe said distractedly, eyes on the radio. "What is this shit?" he muttered, with his bushy eyebrows raised in confusion.

"Oasis. A band. They're English." The song ended. After a station identification, Britney Spears began to shriek through the tinny speakers. Poe winced like he had bitten his tongue.

"Switch it. Please."

McRay fiddled with the radio until he came on the oldies station and left it there. He ignored Poe's distasteful hand gesture in response to this latest, subtle joke. "Superbad Part II" began to play, and both McRay and Poe lapsed into silence while the hardest working man in show business got on with it. Neither wanted to admit that they actually liked the song.

"Edwards was with us in the service," Poe abruptly stated as they pulled into a gated complex of cheap, stuccoed apartment buildings. "Since then he's been out of the game."

"So he's in from way back, huh?" McRay asked, unholstering his backup pistol and checking the action. The smooth, matte-black Glock clacked satisfyingly into place.

"One of the good ol' boys," Poe said. "Now he's a cop. He's in on the Lumsden case. He notified . . . well, we were notified, okay? And now we're here. The end."

Poe slipped the Ford Taurus into an open slot, next to the super's space in front of a tarpaulin-laden pool covered in frozen clumps of dead leaves. To their right lay a double tier of apartments decorated in early American crap. Discarded hibachis, old Big Wheels, rotted-out tin drums and abandoned, sun-washed Fisher Price toys were scattered about the frozen lawn like inner city dandruff.

Poe pulled a hatbox-sized pack from the back seat. He'd retrieved it from the airport locker, and now he unfolded it like a bathroom kit. Four guns were in the case, held in place by black Velcro straps. Three were small black numbers—Berettas, probably, though McRay wouldn't bet his lunch on it—and the fourth barely fit from side to side in the confines of the package.

"Aces," Poe smiled. "Deb came through."

McRay watched in silence as Poe removed the largest handgun in the bunch and checked the action, then loaded and cocked it. Poe shoved it in an interior jacket pocket where it hung, pendulous, like an enormous piece of tribal jewelry. He stepped from the car and McRay stepped out as well, chucking his half-eaten bag of Fritos to the bucket of the front seat. They quietly shut their doors. McCray found himself staring at Poe.

"Did you want to ask me something, Curtis?" Poe whispered, his eyes on the upper tier of the apartments, face somber.

"No-o-o-o-sir," McRay replied looking at the gun's profile in Poe's jacket.

"Don't say anything until I introduce you. Eddie is a bit . . . jumpy."

"The guy's name is Eddie Edwards?" McRay croaked, mostly to himself.

Poe brought a single finger up to his lips and whispered, *Shhhh*.

They went up.

EDDIE EDWARDS LOOKED LIKE shit.

When Edwards opened the door and considered the two new arrivals, McRay could tell he had been up for some time, and that he had something pointing at them out of sight beyond the door.

It turned out to be a sawed-off shotgun.

The little sweat-stained man swung the door wide when he saw Poe but said nothing. He didn't even look at McRay. The two men hurried in from the cold. Edwards closed the door and placed the shotgun down on an already overfilled coffee table. Stacks of photocopies and various newspapers teetered on the edge of collapse as the table shook; but somehow, everything on it remained precariously balanced. The room smelled like cigarette smoke and stale beer. Unsure of the protocol, McRay remained standing near the door.

Poe thumped down on an ancient, stained couch that squeaked like old bedsprings and let out a grunt as Edwards disappeared into a bedroom. Poe removed his enormous pistol and placed it on the overfilled table, where it too failed to knock down the delicately constructed mess.

Edwards returned with two old mugs full of steaming coffee and handed one to each of them.

Poe downed half of it in one go and then looked at McRay, who took a small swig to please his audience, miming appreciation. The cup read "Crazy + Gullible = Happy" in plain black writing.

"This is Cyrus," Poe said, pointing at McRay, using his conspiracy name. "He's good people".

Edwards nodded towards McRay and then looked earnestly at Poe.

"This is some serious shit going on here, Poe," Edwards croaked.

"Tell us," said McRay.

So Edwards did.

MICHAEL ANTHONY LUMSDEN, AGE nine or nineteen depending on what you believed, was found asleep in his pajamas in the kitchen of his parents' home the morning of January 24, 2001. The problem with this heart-warming story was that Michael Lumsden had died from childhood leukemia at age nine, and was buried ten years and three months, almost to the day, before his discovery in his parent's kitchen.

He had not aged at all since his apparent death. Apparently healthy and full of good cheer, the nine-year-old acted as if nothing untoward had occurred. He could not recall exactly how he had gotten home or where he had been before. He did not recall his illness or lengthy hospital stay. To him, it was still 1990.

The Lumsdens did little to interfere with this belief. The boy's flabbergasted mother nearly had a stroke when she saw the child for the first time. Then she and her husband started calling loved ones. It was at this time that the Lumsdens discovered their other son, Bob, a graduate student at Rutgers University, was missing. Torn between joy and worry, the Lumsdens plodded on as best they could. The New Brunswick police were informed of Bob Lumsden's disappearance and the boy's father traveled to New Jersey to look into the disappearance. Nothing came of it and he returned home.

The Bob Lumsden case was still open.

There was no doubt in the Lumsdens' minds that the little boy who had suddenly appeared in the kitchen was their son, Michael. He had extensive, personal knowledge of the family. He knew family secrets and details no stranger could know.

The mother, Rosemarie Lumsden, insisted that the family doctor Frank Wainwright examine Michael at length, to be sure there was no sign of leukemia. It was then the police became involved. The stunned Doctor Wainwright, who had treated Michael in the past and who clearly recognized the child, informed the authorities of the bizarre nature of his patient. Quite at a loss for what to do, he simply requested that the police look into the matter.

The Philadelphia Police Department sent detectives. No crime could be discerned. They suspected some sort of scenario with a deranged mother abducting another family's child, but no child matching the description of "Michael Lumsden" had been reported missing. The boy himself believed he was Michael Lumsden and could not be swayed from this belief. Michael's fingerprints were run against a set taken from him at age four in 1985. They were an exact match. Dental records matched as well. DNA from hair samples was being tested even now, but so far everything pointed to the fact that Michael Lumsden had somehow risen from the grave.

The police suggested that Rosemarie keep the incident as quiet as possible while higher-ups in the city government looked for guidance, but things as strange as this, rare as they were, had a habit of spilling out. Though the detectives on the case still believed it to be a kidnapping and brainwashing, the sudden media attention, along with the Lumsdens' cooperation with the authorities, made the police very nervous. One misstep could open the department to a huge lawsuit and a media-spun PR nightmare. The mayor made the call: Wait until more information was uncovered. Don't move until the identity of "Michael Lumsden" could be established.

"Michael" was kept under lock and key at the Lumsden house and the police assigned a dozen men to watch the home, four men in each shift, around the clock.

"I'm in on the case and I've got access to the reports," Edwards said. "They forgot one thing."

Poe placed his coffee down on the cluttered table and asked, with an air of regret, "What's that, Eddie?"

"They were so busy trying to figure out who the kid was, they forgot to check the coffin."

Despite the warmth of the coffee and the fog of it steaming his glasses, McRay felt something cold unfold in his gut. He now realized what the shovels, work gloves and tarp piled in the corner were for.

Busy, Busy

Initial police interview in the disappearance of Robert M. Lumsden: New Brunswick, New Jersey. 40.48 N/74.46 W latitude/longitude. Approximately 54 miles from Philadelphia, Pennsylvania: Sunday, January 28, 2001, 3:02 P.M. EST.

SHOVED INTO A SUIT two years too small for his current girth and twelve years out of date, Vincent Garrity tried his best to smile at the two detectives. It didn't work. His face was fixed in a grimace, the expression of a man trying to pass an inordinately large gallstone. And then there was the sweating. Less than half an hour into the interview his suit was soaked through the back and under the arms, and he kept wiping his brow with a wrist that was already dripping wet. He knew it didn't look good. He was no idiot. He was a scientist.

Both detectives looked blandly amused with his performance. They stared at him calmly and occasionally would start in with rapid, cross-referenced questions, hoping to trip him up. They didn't, but the interview dragged on. The last half hour seemed longer than the last year of his life.

"So, Vincent. One more time, huh? We're not all that up on this high-tech stuff." Detective Grogan sighed. He scratched his short white hair and then considered the papers on the desk as if reading some relevant fact.

Garrity was sure this was all just an act. Beyond the two detectives his fat reflection stared back in the two-way mirror, comically frightened. No matter how hard he concentrated, he couldn't seem to get the expression off his face. On the other side of that mirror, he was certain, others were watching the session, taping it, even. Maybe. Was there a law against that in this state? He would have to look it up.

"Yeah," Detective Orville said through cigarette-stained teeth.

"My kids on the computer, same thing—mouse this, fax that . . . who knows?"

"We're old-fashioned guys," Grogan laughed, eyeing Garrity with a smile that said, *Laugh along, we're friends.* But Garrity didn't laugh. He had never felt so somber in his entire life.

"So, yeah, what Detective Grogan is asking is, what's this thingamajob you and Lumsden were working on?"

Garrity cleared his throat and leaned forward.

"I already told you."

"So tell us again," Grogan said quietly.

"Please," Orville finished.

"The Passive Brain State Monitor and Display," Garrity said.

"Yeah, that thing." Grogan smiled.

"What does it do again?" Orville inquired softly, fixing Garrity with a cold glance.

"It . . . well, do you know the MRI?"

"Um . . . that's that magnetic doohickey they use at the hospital, right?"

"Yes," Garrity said. "The PBSMD is like that . . . um . . . sort of, except for the brain. It monitors the brain's state through non-invasive means." He looked up into two blank stares.

"It uses an MRI of the brain and the computer projects the brain state, designated by color code on a screen which the patient can look at and. . . ."

Blank stares.

"Have you ever heard of biofeedback?" Garrity felt trapped, out of his league and superior in the same moment. He felt crazy.

"No," the two detectives said in unison.

"Well. Um." Garrity considered the damp hand that he had just swept across his brow. His fingers were trembling.

"Go on."

"Biofeedback is a teaching loop. Um. It lets normal people control functions that aren't usually under conscious control."

"Like?"

"Heartbeat, blood flow, brainwave activity—which is what me and Bob were working on. Other things as well—"

Orville interrupted. "How does this . . . work?" Grogan looked through him, letting his boredom slip through his mask of efficiency for just a moment. Garrity thought that boredom was a good thing. You didn't get bored when you were going in for the kill. Maybe this really was just an informal interview.

"You hook a machine up to a patient to say, um, monitor their heart rate, and the machine chimes at every heartbeat so the patient can hear it. Now the patient knows whether or not his heartbeat is going faster or slower due to the, um, tone, so he can slowly gain control over it. He can make it go faster or slower, at will."

The two detectives looked at each other over the table.

"There's a lot of money in this, huh, Vince?" Grogan asked.

"Eventually. Maybe," Garrity admitted.

"How maybe?" Orville asked.

"Well it depends on how good the device is. So far, it's been giving us some . . . um, troubles."

"Troubles?"

"Computer glitches. Nothing unusual."

"Lumsden's problems?"

"Uh. No, Earl Mitchell handles the computer stuff."

"I see. So who owns the idea?"

"I do," Garrity said, feeling a warm sense of pride in his chest despite the fear. It was his idea, after all.

"So Lumsden didn't own any of it?"

"No. I involved Lumsden and, um, Mitchell and Loew after I designed it. I have paperwork. It's, um, well documented."

"So what did Lumsden do for you, then?"

"All the guys are graduate students, um, like me, in different fields at the U. Lumsden was a component engineer. He built the PBSMD from my specifications—"

"Yeah. And Loew was the medical guy and Mitchell was the computer guy, right?"

"Yes."

There was a moment of silence.

"You're free to go, Mr. Garrity," Orville finally said, sounding perplexed.

"Yeah, you look . . . ready to get out of here." Grogan smiled.

"Yeah, I have a lot to do," Garrity said. "I've got to stay busy, um . . . busy."

"But don't go anywhere."

"Nope, nowhere to go," Garrity replied, shaken.

But they didn't have anything on him.

None of the others had said a word about the incident. After that night, he had expected Loew to spill it—it seemed a secret too big for anyone to contain, even for a short time. He could feel it in him even now, an overwhelming urge to shout out the truth, to scream what happened to Bob Lumsden at the top of his lungs. It was the most amazing thing he had ever seen in his life, even if it only was on video. Perhaps the most amazing thing to ever occur in all of human history. But he kept his mouth shut and left the two detectives to their plotting. He had reams of raw data to examine, and if what he believed had happened to Lumsden could happen again. . . .

He was free. Free, for now. Soon he hoped to be more free than any human being in history—except one.

He believed that he and he alone had the tool that would make it possible to find Bob Lumsden.

Not Who . . . What

The conspiracy goes into action: Serenity Hills Cemetery, Philadelphia, Pennsylvania. 39.93 N/75.18 W latitude/longitude. Approximately 54 miles from New Brunswick, New Jersey: Monday, January 31, 2001, 12:09 A.M. EST.

SERENITY HILLS CEMETERY WAS an endless expanse of bone-white gravestones reflecting the cold moon like a million lidless eyes. It rode two hillsides in Roxborough and looked down on the Schuylkill River, which wound in the valley below like a twisting beam of light. It was silent and isolated.

But not empty.

As they pulled into the parking lot, McRay spied a large Cadillac de Ville idling near a darkened gatehouse with a plume of smoke rising out of its exhaust. As they pulled in, McRay saw the red wink of a cigarette tip in the shadow of the car.

"Shit, someone's here," McRay said, pointing.

Edwards leaned forward between the seats and grabbed Poe's shoulder. "I know them. It's cool."

Poe gave McRay a sideways glance and the skinny man unbuttoned his coat and loosened his gun from his shoulder rig. He clicked the safety off. He nodded to Poe who pulled in a few spaces from the de Ville. Edwards piled out of the car and walked over to the de Ville. A shadow lumbered from the car to join him. They shook hands.

"How well do you know Edwards?" McRay whispered.

"Pretty well," Poe said, but checked his own pistol anyway.

Edwards waved them over.

"Here it goes," Poe murmured, and stepped from the car. He left it running.

McRay stepped out, too, but kept low behind the mass of the

car, watching the three men talk quietly about fifty feet away. He saw, or thought he saw, a brick-sized envelope change hands. It was a payoff of some sort.

Poe waved and McRay trotted over.

The stranger was obviously connected. He was wearing a cashmere sweater beneath a nine hundred dollar Bergdorf Goodman long coat, shoes worth more than a used car, and a watch that would choke a jeweler. His teeth were blindingly white and his hair was a deep, unnatural black. He grinned as McRay walked up, and offered his hand. It glittered with gaudy gold and silver rings. The stranger was the smallest man present and he appeared to be alone, but he seemed comfortable despite the circumstances.

McRay shook a hand that was dry and smelled of talcum.

Edwards continued his conversation.

"So, no problems?"

"None," the man smiled.

"Good, good. We done, then?"

The stranger fumbled in his bulky jacket for a moment. Seeing McRay and Poe both tense up, he froze and laughed, removing his hands from his jacket slowly and then holding them high in a mock gesture of surrender. He pulled his jacket open to show he carried no weapons and again smiled that sickening smile.

"I'm sorry. I just have a map for you." He carefully plucked a paper from an interior breast pocket. It looked like a photocopy of a sheet from the cemetery management company; a highlighted path in yellow marker was traced from the front gates to lot 1611, grave 41. Lumsden, Michael, 1980–1990.

Edwards took it. "Thanks."

"My pleasure. Say hi to J.P.," the little man said over his shoulder as he got back into his de Ville. He lit another cigarette and pulled away.

"Who's J.P.?" Poe asked when stranger had gone.

"The chief of detectives. My boss," Edwards said, walking back to the rental car.

"Good to know," Poe replied.

The three men popped the trunk and removed their gear. They disappeared into the sea of graves.

WHEN THEY ARRIVED AT the lot marked on the map, they discovered a small, gas-powered backhoe parked next to a freshly dug—or more precisely, re-dug—grave. The frozen chunks of dirt removed by the machine were piled neatly beside it on a canvas tarp. Next to them on a second carefully placed tarp were fourteen pieces of fresh sod, slowly freezing in the night air.

Four new shovels were neatly laid out in a line with the tags still on them.

At the head of the grave a modest piece of marble proclaimed it to be the final resting site of Michael Lumsden's earthly remains. McRay and the others had their doubts; he could tell by the glint in their eyes, the same look he was sure was on his own face.

Edwards shone a keychain flashlight into the hole.

"We got about a foot to go. They dug it out to below the permafrost. Otherwise, we'd be digging 'til we puked."

"Just like '68, only colder," Poe said, and the two men set to digging with the folding shovels they brought from the car. McRay kept watch, huddled down into a ball against the cold. The graveyard was silent and still. No wind, no animals, no people, it looked as dead and uninviting as the surface of the moon.

McRay jumped at the hollow report of the shovel striking the lid of the coffin. By then he had been lost in his own thoughts and was far, far away from the graveyard and the cold. The sound brought him back suddenly.

He glanced down into the dark hole and saw two shadows struggling with the lid of a silver coffin. The sports model, he nonsensically thought, and shivered. Graves and graveyards gave him the creeps. It was the one fear that had remained with him throughout his life, from his earliest memories until today, completely unchanged. After what he had seen with the conspiracy, most other fears seemed somehow shallow, whatever power they once held over him. Not graveyards. They still held his mind in check.

So he turned and continued his vigil, trying to push the fear away. With some effort the men in the hole smashed the lock and opened the lid. The sounds echoed through the hills. McRay was tempted to ask them to keep it down but he knew, deep down, that it would do no good. It was necessary. Murmuring continued from the two men, and then he heard the sound of a flimsy, filmlike material being handled. A bright light ignited in the hole.

The talking went on for a while but was too low to be understood. All in all, McRay was happy to be where he was. He wanted as little to do with the grave as possible. But something black within him wanted to know. Who was in that coffin? Could it possibly be Michael Lumsden? Only snippets of the conversation were intelligible. Suddenly it ended and the light clicked off. The coffin lid slammed shut.

Hands appeared on the lip of the grave and for a second McRay was filled with a white-hot terror that rose like molten bile in his throat. They were bone-white hands, grasping for purchase on the frozen ground—

McRay then realized they were just gloves, the rubber gloves Poe had worn.

Poe pulled himself out of the hole clumsily. Edwards followed.

The three of them filled in the grave in silence. They threw in the frozen bits of permafrost first, and then tamping down the last bits of dirt with the tips of their shovels to smooth it out. When they were done Edwards laid out the pieces of sod over the churned dirt. The tampering looked minimal, now, except for the lump of dirt, but it would be noticed if anyone came along to look.

Still silent, they walked back to the car and drove Edwards home.

"So?" McRay broke the silence first on the drive away from Edwards' place.

"So what?" Poe's eyes were fixed on the road.

"So was it Lumsden in the hole?"

"Yeah," Poe barked, turning to look McRay in the eyes for a moment. Then he looked away.

"Are you sure?"

"Yes! Eddie checked his fuckin' little teeth," Poe said. "He had bad teeth, the kid," he added sadly. Little more than a whisper.

"So . . . who is at the Lumsden house right now? Who are the cops guarding?"

"Not who. What."

McRay didn't need to ask what he meant. They both already knew more about what than they cared to.

"What," Poe repeated, quietly, to himself.

They drove further into the dark.

This *X-Files* Shit

Phenomen-X *gets a call: Culver City, Los Angeles, California. 34.05 N/118.24 W latitude/longitude. Approximately 2,400 miles from Philadelphia, Pennsylvania: Monday, January 31, 2001, 12:03 P.M. PST.*

"Do you know who this is?" the voice on the line asked.

Frank Carincola shut his door, only barely dampening the sounds of the busy studio floor below. The plasterboard walls in the rickety warehouse were paper-thin. They were in the middle of taping the weekly episode of his baby, the syndicated cable show *Phenomen-X*, and the crew was raising hell between takes, shifting equipment from here to there. Sonja was yelling at someone about something and Tommy Prendergast was laughing. Finally something huge and probably expensive fell to the cement floor with a crash. Curses and shouts floated up. Carincola winced and looked down but could see nothing amiss through the Levolor blinds; only a half-dozen people conferring in a small circle in the middle of the floor. Damn, did that ever sound expensive, he thought, and tried to gather his nerve.

"Yes, I know who this is," Carincola replied distractedly. "What have you got?" His bald head hung low as he listened. His shirt was unbuttoned and dirty and his thick bifocal glasses were smeared with grime. To the average person he would have looked terrible, but in the paranoid life of Frank Carincola this was a good day. He was doing pretty well. He was just dandy.

He hadn't even picked up his gun today. Well, not really. He had held it, but he hadn't pointed it at anybody.

Yet.

"Fideles, Arizona, two miles south-southwest of Dreamland," the voice stated. "Be there tomorrow. This is the most important event of the century. Watch the skies. Wait. Be patient."

A rap at the door made him jump, and by the time he had shifted around the desk to unlock it the line had gone dead. A dial tone droned in his ear like a warning.

"Damn," Carincola said, and hung up the phone.

"Sir?" Tommy Prendergast entered the room sheepishly. He wore a beaten *Phenomen-X* cap and a *Batman: The Dark Knight* T-shirt. His moon-like, pimpled face was full of interest. He saw the expression on Carincola's face and froze. Tommy was well versed in his boss' paranoid excesses. The spackled bullet holes in the wall told the tale.

"Yes. Yes, Tommy, what is it?"

"Miss Dewey just hit Mister Carmichael and Mister Harris just walked out."

"Okay, Tommy. I'll be down in a sec." Carincola jotted down Fideles, Arizona on a note pad and then considered the map on the wall. He slid a red pushpin on the dot that represented Fideles, lost in the middle of the endless desert of the southwest. The map was full of them, now, some red, some blue; but the mark at Fideles was hundreds of miles from any other pin or town. Carincola wondered if that meant something. It was a few seconds before he realized Tommy was still there, waiting. The kid's eyes were on the pad and then they slid to the map.

"Thanks, Tommy, you can go."

The kid vanished instantly. Carincola returned to his squeaky chair (his throne, Sonja called it) and put his head in his hands. After a while he slid open his desk drawer, pulled out his snub-nose .38, and quickly checked it. It was fully loaded.

"Oh God, I am so fucking sick of this *X-Files* shit," he said to no one at all, and picked up the phone. He had some reservations to make.

Δ

Poe hung up the phone. He looked across the sterile hotel room at McRay, who sat with his legs up on a small sofa. Their gear was scattered around the room, trying to assert some type of personality on its blandness. But the gear was no match for the paintings of anonymous ponds full of ducks, and the tan-and-green color scheme of the walls that had been in vogue for thirty seconds sometime in the mid-Seventies. Everything in the room had been scoured clean of meaning by ten thousand mornings of the shades being drawn open on the day after. Everything looked fake and old.

Except for the FedEx package. The red and blue on the box were vibrant, the only vibrant color in the room except for McRay's eyes. It was hard not to look at that color.

Poe's newly received shipment of equipment from Virginia lay open on the bed. Inside, packed in molded foam, was disassembled matte-black death.

"Well?" McRay asked.

"A-Cell's taken care of the Fourth Estate—at least, our equivalent of the Fourth Estate. They'll be chasing their tails in Arizona while we do our thing."

"Good deal," McRay smiled. "I can't stand those fuckin' guys."

Memories swept into the spotlight of his mind without warning. A spray of images like knives falling from the air, each aiming for the heart. *Fumbling with his pistol in a darkened bathroom. Something slinking up his arm like warm Jell-O. Poe shouting and emptying an MP5 at men dressed in black suits in a wheat field. A man's head exploding like a grapefruit filled with an M-80. Shasta tackling McRay and shouting a warning to Poe and Ulysses. Black helicopters. The hospital stay, super-flu and purple dye. Groversville, oh God, Groversville and death—*

"To Groversville," Poe offered, interrupting McRay's internal rehashing of past, and therefore unimportant, events. The big man held up his sanitized-for-your-protection cup full of airline gin in a mock toast and smiled a smile like lemons.

"To Francis and Ulysses," McRay somberly replied, trying to remember their faces, what their last words had been. Instead he could only recall the metallic taste of his own fear and the sound of men screaming.

Neither one of them mentioned Shasta.

The two men drank in silence for a long time.

"Are we going to do what I think we're going to do?" McRay finally asked.

Poe didn't answer. He just stood and began to assemble his weapon. That was all the answer McRay needed.

Conduits

Class One paranormal event: Snohomish Medical Examiner's Office, Snohomish, Washington. 47.91 N/122.27 W Latitude/Longitude. Approximately 2,382 miles from New Brunswick, New Jersey: Sunday, January 28, 2001, 11:44 P.M. PST.

TWO LARGE, OVERHEAD LAMPS starkly lit the metal tray where the body lay. A hundred scratched and glittering autopsy tools traced an 'L' around the table, carefully laid out in trays on white paper. Fleetwood Mac played on a small clock radio on a shelf of well-thumbed medical textbooks. Walter Smith, the chief prosector, stood next to it, hands frozen in the air with a perplexed expression on his plump face. His mouth was pursed and his eyebrows were scrunched down. The long, hook-like prosector's knife hung forgotten in one of his hands. Walter Smith didn't quite understand what he was seeing.

Smith was not prone to flights of fancy. He was a dour man who was disliked by his colleagues (it was no secret) but he did his job well and by the book. When you had little else in life it was easy to learn to love one's work. Even if it did involve dealing with bodies like that of Moriarity, Timothy M., the one lying in front of him.

Something had subjected the body to terrible forces. From the lowest rib upward the upper half of the torso was scraped clean to bone and gristle, like a man dragged for a mile over raw gravel. The internal organs seemed to be intact, but until the autopsy began there was no way to really tell. Moriarity's eyes were gone, as was most of his face. No ears, no scalp, no nose. From the torso up Moriarity was just a mass of dried, bloody bits, now nearly defrosted after days in the freezer. Worse yet, many of the wounds seemed to have begun to clot in an attempt to heal, indicating that Moriarity had been alive for several hours while it—whatever it was that happened—happened.

Below the chest, the rest of the body was untouched, as neat as a portion of wall that a painter has taped off to keep it clean. Moriarity's trousers were covered in blood, but they were not affected otherwise. His sneakers were completely clean.

All in all, it was a bizarre case. But this was not what confused Dr. Smith. There were many possible explanations for these things: dragging, a fall, other things. There was always an explanation. It was his job to determine the cause. He dealt with the dead. They spoke to him. Metaphorically, that is. They could not gesture or move or talk.

Most of all, occasional rigor aside, they did not move.

What could possibly explain what he was seeing now? Smith's mind was idling in neutral while things happened in front of him. It was mesmerizing. Science had no immediate answers for what he was seeing, only supposition, and rather outré supposition at that. Somehow, right now, supposition did not seem like enough.

The ruined and scraped skin of Moriarity's solar plexus was slowly expanding and contracting. Hardly even noticeable, really. But he had noticed it, just seconds before he planned to insert the prosector's knife into the spot which was now—what was it doing? It looked almost like . . . almost like . . . like, well, breathing. But the body had been in a freezer for more than five days. Moriarity was definitely dead. No one could possibly survive the injuries he had been subjected to, not to mention a prolonged stay in deep freeze. But what else could it be? The years of instructions, the hundreds of books he had read to bring him to this job remained silent in Walter Smith's mind.

Insects, maybe? An unnoticed animal? A rat? Gas?

What could possibly survive in a freezer for five days?

Silence.

Suddenly Dr. Smith felt very alone. He was here after hours to finish the job on Timothy Moriarity as a personal favor to another overworked examiner, topping off an already overloaded schedule with the coup de grace of this bizarre case. He always got the unusual ones. Everyone had filtered out hours ago, heading home. To watch television. To eat dinner. To sleep a sleep of comfort and safety behind locked and familiar doors.

Smith wished he were home right now.

The movement continued, and Smith stepped carefully back to the wall phone. One light on the bank of switches at its base was blinking. It was marked 'CUST.' Smith pressed it down and lifted the receiver. A conversation was going on between the janitor and another party about the upcoming Super Bowl.

"Mister . . . " Smith began, eyes never leaving the corpse. Suddenly, he could not recall the janitor's name. "Rudel?" he finished, more a question than a statement. The janitor and the other party stopped speaking immediately.

"Yes sir?" the janitor asked. "I got to go, Bud," he said to the other person on the line. There was a click as Bud hung up.

"Can you come down to the autopsy room, please?"

"I'm sorry for talking on the phone, Dr. Smith. I know—"

"That's not what this is about. I need—" I need to be home in bed, he thought to himself, but he finished: "—help down here."

"Oh?" There was no real surprise in Rudel's voice, only relief. "Okay."

The light on the phone clicked off.

The movement in the corpse continued. Dr. Smith's mind began to rattle off explanations, but each sounded less believable than the last.

When Burt Rudel pushed through the double doors into the autopsy room, Smith shouted in surprise and dropped the receiver he had forgotten to hang up. It struck the wall with a hollow plastic sound.

"Sorry there, doc," Rudel said, and shrugged. "What'd you—" He froze, eyeing the corpse. His eyes slowly widened until they seemed to be bulging from the sockets.

Dr. Smith felt a wave of relief as he realized Rudel saw it as well.

"What the fuck?" Rudel said in a high disbelieving voice.

The skin seemed to bulge as if reacting to the noise of Rudel's voice. Smith could not be sure, but it seemed to push in Rudel's direction. That can't be possible, he thought to himself. This isn't happening. The thoughts were comforting but false, and he knew it. This was real. This was happening. *The real world is real; we know, because things we do not wish to happen in it happen all the time,* a ghostly voice intoned in his mind. Who had said that?

"I don't know what it is," Dr. Smith said, staring at the corpse. The two men continued to speak without looking at each other. "Do we have any rat problems you know of, Mr. Rudel?"

"No, sir."

"I'm going to cut it open."

"I don't think that's such a good idea. Maybe—"

A convulsive flexing of the body cut off Rudel. It jumped at least seven inches off the steel table before crashing down again. The sound was huge in the tile-covered room. Smith backed up to the wall with his mouth hanging open and Rudel took two steps back to the double doors. The bulge at the solar plexus was now a stretched, ruined pimple of skin the size of tea saucer. It looked ready to burst, to let forth a stream of—what? The skin around the bulge was stretched like punched leather, and tiny blue-red splits were visible on its surface.

"It's like fuckin' *Alien.* Sigourney Weaver. Just like it," Rudel said. He crossed himself, backing up. Smith took two bold steps to the autopsy tools and snatched up a pair of surgical shears, discarding the prosector's knife on the shelf. He leapt back just as quickly: the skin shifted to the left, towards his movement.

"That ain't no rat," Rudel whispered, and the doctor nodded his head. Something in his mind told him to run away. But that voice was dim and indistinct, and it went against everything he had ever been taught. He held the surgical shears out in front of him like some holy item, some mystical symbol of science that could ward off whatever was inside the corpse. Rudel snatched a mallet from a table for processing bone fragments, and took one step forward. The two men were less than four feet from the body when it moved again.

The body began to tremble on the table, slowly at first, but soon enough the movement was so violent that the tools on the trays next to it jittered and shook to the ground in a clattering cascade, spilling everywhere. A large scalpel dropped into the rubber-tiled floor, sticking straight up, impaled in the mat like a steel exclamation point. Smith couldn't be sure, but over the ruckus he thought he heard Rudel screaming, a crazed disbelieving keening, like a dog being beaten, like he was trying to stop the body's spasms through his screams. The corpse trembled for more than a minute as they watched, fascinated and horrified. Then it stopped suddenly, like a current within it had been switched off by some invisible source. Rudel stopped screaming with it.

In the silence that followed, the clicking of the clock sounded very loud.

"Rudel, get that camera on the shelf, next to the sink," Smith whispered. "The uh, camcorder." He gestured toward the far corner of the room, a point past the body on the table, on the other side of . . . whatever it was.

Rudel shook his head slowly. "No, sir," he said. "Not for ten fifty an hour. Not for a thousand fifty an hour, neither."

The two men stood there for some time, frozen, unsure what

to do.

"I tell you what, doc," Rudel said finally in a squeaking, pleading whisper. "I'm going home. This ain't normal, here. If I get fired, well, I find another job. Nope, that's not so bad. . . ." Rudel's face had gone ashen. His eyebrows were moving up and then down again repetitively, but his eyes remained wide, like a man struggling to see underwater. Smith thought Rudel looked crazy, as he watched the man's face contort and push in on itself to project feelings it was not used to expressing. He looked like an inmate at an asylum.

Rudel's mouth worked open and closed, but Smith suddenly realized that for some reason words had ceased coming out. Rudel goggled like a grounded fish. Like he couldn't catch his breath. Smith felt something black and cold seep into his stomach as he realized Rudel's eyes were still fixed on the surgical table and his were not.

Smith looked.

The ruined body of Timothy M. Moriarity was sitting up on the table, staring at them with empty, eyeless sockets.

THE SHELLS OF THE pistol recovered at the scene of Timothy Moriarity's murder were in storage when they began to move. Each had been tagged, bagged and numbered on the 26th, the night the body was discovered, and they resided from that point on in an evidence locker in the Snohomish County Sheriff's Office. This locker was in a secured room in the basement of the building. It was rarely entered except for very specific and well-monitored reasons.

No one was present when each shell began to shift and roll and burst, one by one, like party favors that spewed out not confetti but small, crustacean-like creatures. Each creature was about the size of a flea, with a random assortment of pinchers, legs and limbs. Most were covered in tiny, unblinking eyes. When each shell had opened and spewed its brood, the creatures carefully arranged themselves in a small pile, climbing and interlocking in a precarious balancing act. When the last of the creatures arrived in its preordained spot, the group froze.

The pile remained undisturbed for four hours while the creatures within it went through various changes, just as they were designed to.

The hole in the evidence locker was discovered the next day. It led to a brief but general confusion as to what could have possibly caused such a large tear in the 3/4-gauge steel. When the tapes from the surveillance video camera poised at the door of the room were reviewed, no one was seen coming or going. And although it was noticed that the hole seemed to be punched from the inside out, no one could offer any explanation.

Nothing unusual was found in the room.

THE SAME EVENING, THE manager and owner of the Tesoro gas station, Eduard Hadid, fielded the phone call from his couch while watching a taped NASCAR race on his widescreen television. The voice on the other end of the line was yelling, and it took a moment or two before Hadid realized it was one of the contractors he had hired to re-install the door to his Snohomish station. For some reason, the nut who had murdered one of his clerks had found it necessary to tile up the doorway to his service station. Crazies were everywhere, these days. Crazies cost money.

Now there was a damn problem with the contractor. What next?

"Calm down," Hadid managed, speaking in the starts and gaps of the babbling man's speech. "What is going on there? Hello?"

"Mr. Hadid, you better get down here! Something's come up."

"What now?" Hadid groaned, envisioning a number followed by a limitless number of zeros: the bill.

"Um, we started taking the wall down, yeah? To put—oh fuck, you tell him," the man said, exasperated. Hadid heard the phone shift hands.

"Hadid?" a gruff voice said.

"Yes?"

"Hadid, we have a problem. One of my workmen put a nice-sized hole in your wall, and. . . ." The gruff voice died off into confused mumbling.

"Yes, go on?" Hadid replied, annoyed.

"It began to bleed," the man finished.

It took Eduard Hadid more than twenty seconds to come to terms with what the caller had said.

Done and Done

The conspiracy hopes to gain the high ground: Days Inn, 2221 Highway 76, Philadelphia, Pennsylvania. 39.93 N/75.18 W latitude/longitude. Approximately 2,374 miles from Seattle: Thursday, February 1, 2001, 10:29 A.M. EST.

THEY SAT IN A generic restaurant that was attached to the side of the Days Inn like a stucco parasite. Poe drank cup after cup of black coffee as McRay scanned the parking lot through the window. Out on Highway 76, cars and trucks trundled by, reflecting back the unseasonably bright sun.

"When is he coming again?" McRay asked, pushing his plate away. The French toast on it was cooling and untouched.

"Edwards said he has to put in some time. People are getting suspicious," Poe grunted through a mouthful of toast. He waved the waiter over with a humungous hand. Coffee was poured in silence.

"So? When's he due?" McRay said as he laid his head on his arms and closed his eyes.

"Soon. What's the story on the Buffalo office? Are you due back soon?"

"The week after next," McRay sighed. "As far as they know I'm still in St. Thomas." He glanced out the window once more as a car pulled up, but it was not Edwards. "St. Thomas . . . " McRay repeated, his eyes far away.

Poe pulled McRay's plate over to his side of the table and started eating the partially congealed French toast and syrup with fervor. They sat in silence for some time, watching the few cars pull in and out of the lot with interest. In less than five minutes Poe had decimated the plate of French toast, leaving only a sprig of some wilted and unidentified green behind.

"What did A-Cell have to say?" McRay finally asked.

"The same as they always do," Poe laughed, and then belched. An old woman two tables down glanced around, frowning. When she saw the immense form of Poe smiling back at her she quickly turned back to her meal.

"Which is?"

"If you don't know that by now, kid, you are in for some serious shit." Poe smiled.

McRay looked up. "I know what they said. I just want to hear it."

"They said, 'Take care of it,' " Poe muttered, looking away.

"Is it just me, or does it feel like we're the only ones who ever do?"

"What's going on with you, McRay? You losing your faith?" Poe's expression didn't change.

"I just don't know how cool I'll be when it comes down to . . . what we have to do." McRay tried not to meet the big man's eyes.

"If it comes to that, I'll take care of it, man," Poe said and waved for the check.

EDWARDS PUSHED INTO THE booth next to McRay at ten past eleven. His shirt was stained and his jacket did not match his pants, but that was not what threw McRay off. Edwards looked awful, and not just in his choice of wardrobe. His eyes were hollow blots of green and his stubbled face was drawn and pale. McRay realized he was very probably looking at a man who was losing his mind. Maybe just in fits and starts—a piece here and there—but McRay was sure it was going somewhere. And wherever that place was, nothing came back from it. He had seen it before. Poe looked unfazed as Edwards sat down.

"Eddie," Poe said.

Edwards looked back. "I came. I kept my promise, Poe. What

do you want? Things are getting hairy. People at the station are looking at me funny." McRay was sure of it, though he was also sure Edwards had no idea how bad he truly looked. Was it possible Edwards' people actually suspected some sort of conspiracy? Or did they just think the guy was losing his marbles?

"Eddie, I need schematics for the house. I also need to know the schedules for the cops who sit watch. If you can get in on a walking tour of the house and case it for me, that would be even better." Poe sipped at his sixth cup of coffee.

Eddie Edwards sat still for a long time.

"Poe, you're not really going to do this, are you? I mean, he's just a kid."

Poe leaned forward and his voice dropped an octave.

"You remember OBSIDIAN? You remember the girl? Oh, she certainly looked like a girl. But was she just a girl, Eddie? Is that what you're telling me? 'Cause if you are, maybe I ought to remind you who saved your ass there. Do you remember, Eddie? Do you? 'Cause I do."

Eddie waved Poe off in a gesture of surrender. The man looked absolutely broken. McRay had no idea what Poe was talking about, but he knew enough to be glad he didn't.

Edwards nodded once and stood. "I'll call you, Poe," he said quietly, and Poe nodded. Edwards drove away in his rotted-out Camaro, heading back into town on Highway 76.

"Done and done," Poe said and stood, dropping two crisp twenties on the scrawled bill.

McRay and Poe left the diner.

There Are Others

Class One paranormal event: New Brunswick, New Jersey. 40.48 N/74.46 W latitude/longitude. Approximately 54 miles from Philadelphia, Pennsylvania: Sunday, February 4, 2001, 3:41 A.M. EST.

VINCENT GARRITY HEARD SOMEONE sit down on his bed. It was the same sound he heard every night, a shuffling, squeaking sound followed by a sigh. Usually he made that sound himself. Tonight, unannounced, someone else was in his apartment.

From the living room, in front of the television on the floor, Garrity could see a pair of ragged red sneakers below the gap in the door to his bedroom. Someone was sitting on his bed. Someone who had not been there a moment before. Someone who had not passed by him to get to the isolated room, and who had presumably not entered through the third-story window in complete silence while Garrity studied data one room away.

Garrity placed the folder down carefully and turned off the mute television.

He got up and pushed the heavy wood door open, slowly. It creaked on its hinges and banged to a halt on the plaster wall. A scattering of dust spilled from the ceiling.

Little more than a shadow, Bob Lumsden sat on the bed in the dark. The room was lit from beams of lamplight that spilled in through the large window from the quad, painted in blues and browns. It was Lumsden, though—that much he could tell just from the slouching posture and the way he held his hands together politely on his lap.

But where had Lumsden gone after hitting Violet 5?

Garrity found his face frozen between a smile and grimace. His body felt hollow, like his whole form was nothing but an eggshell that would crack with any movement. Finally he forced his face into a grin and said, unsteadily:

"Bob?"

Lumsden didn't answer or turn to look. I am seeing a ghost, Garrity thought to himself. This is what it is like; remember this feeling. I created a machine that makes ghosts. The thought brought a wave of nausea and fear that crept up his back and settled into his head like reverberating numbness. He reached out a hand and switched on the light, half expecting Lumsden to vanish.

Instead Lumsden looked up. Thin, ragged and scruffy, he looked precisely the same as when Garrity last saw him. Lumsden smiled a weary smile and there were circles under his eyes. He wore a pullover sweater that was torn at the shoulder, wash-faded jeans, and ratty, ancient, red Converse All-Stars. His hair was a mess and his face was unshaven, probably had been for days.

"I was, uh . . . hoping we could talk, Vince," Lumsden said. He stood up.

Garrity tried his best to control himself, but he slowly backed up to the door, away from Lumsden's forward movement, his eyes feeling inordinately wide. He turned and shut the door behind him rapidly, trying to cover his fear. There was a choice—stay in the room or to run. Garrity could not believe the terror he needed to overcome to stay inside the room. To shut the door. Lumsden watched this all, smiling mildly, his hands raised in a token gesture of peace.

Garrity slowly crossed the room to the rolling chair and sat down. It was the most difficult and frightening thing he had ever done.

"What's . . . what's it like, Bob?" Garrity finally managed.

"It's strange. I can't explain it."

"Try." Garrity leaned forward and placed his elbows on his knees. Lumsden walked to the window and looked out on the quad.

"It's like a song."

They both remained in silence for a moment, and then Lumsden seemed to realize that Garrity did not understand. After a long minute or more of composing his answer, he began to speak again. "This world. This whole universe is just a construct, a notation. Every living thing is simply a focus in these dimensions of something infinite beyond. We . . . well, you . . . are nothing more than a portion of the other world, another dimension, punched through into ours. These bodies are like scuba gear for that intelligence. Your mind is a portion of the other side's infinity, focused into a biological projector that gives it a linear existence. So this infinity can change and shift. This place is incomplete on purpose, so it . . . shifts . . . in patterns . . . like . . . a song. I've gone through. I can go back and forth, now. I can. . . ."

"What? What can you do?" Garrity asked, his voice breaking.

"I thought I could save us all. I hoped I could change things for the better. But I—" Lumsden looked back at Garrity and his face was empty of emotion.

"What?"

"There are Others. Other . . . things there, on the other side. I have yet to meet them, at least in this world. They can do things as well, and I think—I think every time I change things here, everything I affect lets them through. Like I've opened doors I can't close behind me. I'm leaving doors open, is all I'm doing, and things are coming through."

Garrity felt his stomach plummet. *There are Others*, Garrity thought, and felt a new wave of ice fall over his body.

"I've already tried to undo what I've changed, but it doesn't seem to work. Also, I'm beginning to misplace things, to forget things." Lumsden sighed. He pulled the window open and put his head out into the freezing night air. Below on the quad someone was playing music, a simple, driving melody on an acoustic guitar. Lumsden heard it and smiled, listening with obvious relish.

"Springsteen," he said, and leaned out the window. "Not bad, kid," he shouted down.

"What do you—" Garrity began, but Lumsden turned back and cut him off.

"When I'm over there, I can see everything. The whole world frozen at the moment I left, like a perfect, faceted crystal. The whole universe. It's infinity over there. But now, since I've been altering things, when I go back, certain places, those places I affect, those people I change, disappear from my . . . vision. I can't see them anymore, and the blindness is spreading. I think they're changing things, as well. I don't know why. My brother, my family, they're gone. I think maybe I killed them. I'm scared to go back to them . . . to see. . . ."

Lumsden looked down and studied his thin, frail hands, then wrung them in the old familiar Bob Lumsden gesture. Garrity felt something in his mind working hard just to keep up. He was sweating and had to hold his hands taut to his knees so they wouldn't shake.

"What did you want to talk to me about?"

"I want you to destroy the Looking-Glass." Lumsden stated it plainly, considering a beaten CD jewel case.

"Well . . . no. I won't do that, Bob," Garrity said, his voice full of fear.

"I can't do anything more, I can't change anything else. I can't even risk going through anymore, unless I have to. I get the feeling . . . I get the feeling that if I let this go, this all could end. The world. Trust me, destroy the machine, burn the plans and work on something else. Don't make the same mistakes I made."

"We'll figure out what to do together," Garrity began, standing up. Although he was terrified, he found he reached out for Lumsden.

"No. There are a lot of people who would . . . want me for things. There are groups out there right now, trying to find me. I'm not omnipotent or invulnerable. When I'm here I'm just like you, mostly. I'm going to look for a solution on my own. But don't be a fool. Don't mess with the machine anymore. I've learned the hard way that you can't change anything, even when you can."

Lumsden stepped back from Garrity and waved a small, half-handed wave at him. He looked sad and tired and disappointed.

Lumsden faded before Garrity like a photograph being washed out by the sun and filmed in rapid time lapse. The colors of his form became indistinct. His shadow drifted from black to light grey and finally to nothing. He was gone. The rug expanded and settled as his feet and weight disappeared from it.

Garrity stepped through the point in space where Lumsden had been standing and then dropped down onto his messy bed. His mind was racing, full of plans and designs and a future full of himself. Lumsden was greater than human; he was greater than anything ever experienced by humanity.

More than anything else, Garrity wanted that.

If Lumsden was not brave enough to step up to the plate, that was fine. Garrity could handle the job of being God on his own.

Part Two: Life In the Fire

"I watched a snail crawl along the edge of a straight razor. That's my dream; that's my nightmare. Crawling, slithering, along the edge of a straight razor . . . and surviving."

—Colonel Kurtz, *Apocalypse Now*

Unknowns

The Steering Committee meets: The "Country Club," outside Mount Weather, Virginia. 38.98 N/76.50 W latitude/longitude. Approximately 177 miles from New Brunswick, New Jersey: Saturday, February 3, 2001, 4:35 P.M. EST.

"SO WHAT'S THE REPORT on . . . um. What's this thing here about Seattle?" Justin Kroft leveled a steely gaze at the table, a gunslinger out for fresh blood. Thirteen individuals sat at the immaculate table, arguably the most powerful humans on the planet. Kroft stood at head of the table, an unhappy king.

No one's eyes rose to meet his gaze.

Adolph Lepus stood. Dressed in a black suit with his thick, greasy black hair combed back, he looked like an animated corpse, pale as the belly of a day-old fish. He considered the report before him on the polished ebony table, straightened it with one narrow finger so that it was flush with the edge, and began to speak. His voice was high and reedy and contained a Southern twang.

"We've had another incident, sir, like the 1996 Arizona contact. The parasite. You recall?"

Kroft nodded, lowered his steel-framed aviator glasses on his nose and flipped through the report. A grainy photograph of a skinned human body stared back. Its upper torso from the sternum up had been flayed to the bone. The body was standing next to a morgue table in a stiff pose—standing, apparently under its own power. It looked like the photo was a still taken from a surveillance video camera. A time code was in the lower right corner of the image.

"A morgue attendant and a medical examiner were attacked by a . . . ahem . . . corpse on the first of February. We have the security video; Yrjo's boys are dealing with the 'victims' now. The corpse in this case was killed in a manner suggestive of alien technology, something we haven't seen before. We assume that the parasite successfully got a piggy-back on the corpse and fled. We have footage from the security feed of the solar plexus of the corpse moving for some time before the . . . reanimation. It got away clean and it's still on the loose—"

"Um, we are on top of this, though," Gavin Ross interjected, cutting Lepus—his lackey—off. Ross was always forceful but had enough tact not to step on toes, and his lantern jaw rippled as he spoke.

Kroft eyed him with what he hoped was a bland look. Inside, Kroft was plotting. Ross's smile was too bright. Was it possible Kroft had let too much power slip away? NRO Section Delta, the fist inside the glove of MAJESTIC-12, was in the hands of two men under his direction: Ross and Lepus. Together, their names sounded like an omen.

"We have men on the ground there already searching for the sphere," Ross finished, offering a nearly sincere smile for having interrupted.

Kroft sniffed and glanced down at the papers. He then pushed his glasses up his nose fastidiously.

After leveling a withering gaze at Lepus—as if to say, *You let a corpse get away? You idiot.*—Kroft glanced at Lieutenant General Eustis Bell. Bell's round, ashen-brown face held a note of composure, but just a note. Underneath, he looked scared.

"General Bell, did we have any tracks across that area on the. . . ."

"The twenty-sixth of January, sir," Lepus offered.

"Yes, as Adolph says, the twenty-sixth." Kroft lowered himself ponderously into his chair.

Bell stood and adjusted his thin spectacles.

"MOON DUST tracked approximately twenty-four unknown targets over U.S. airspace in that week, sir. Ten have been confirmed as Grey vehicles. Four were over the northwest, three are unknowns." Bell sat and closed his folder.

Kroft asked, "Still no communications from the Greys?"

Bell shook his head. "None."

Kroft grimaced, then cleared his throat. "So it is a possibility we are looking at a parasite situation?"

"I would say so, sir," Lepus answered, after looking at Ross for guidance.

"Have Bostick do a background sweep on the involved parties. They may already be known to us. The Greys are getting bolder in their experiments. I suggest we step up our attempts to discourage them, gentlemen. This may just be another smoke-screen—"

Ross interjected again by raising a huge hand in a 'just a moment' gesture.

"Go ahead, Ross," Kroft murmured.

"Bostick and GARNET are pretty much tied up in the . . . ah . . . rewrite of that June Fort Benning incident."

"I don't remember asking for a status report on GARNET, Ross. I want Bostick on this. Get it done."

"Sir," Ross said, eyes downcast in a proper expression of subjugation. Kroft waved the table away with a contemptuous gesture, like a man displeased with a meal.

The table stood. Kroft stood as well and pointed at Lepus before he could leave. Ross cast a backwards glance at Lepus and Kroft as he exited with the rest, the look of a man going down for what might be the last time. That glance said too much. Kroft could see through that glance into Ross's little mind. That glance said: *Are they plotting against me?*

Good. Things had shifted once more but stalled a precarious

balance. For the moment. These pauses rarely lasted for more than a few weeks at a time.

The door shut. Lepus stood at attention. Kroft turned his back to the thin man and looked out the window at the rolling hills filled with evergreen trees. The untouched parkland that surrounded the Country Club was seamless, except for the razor wire, sensors and NRO DELTA killers wandering its grounds. It was serenity in the midst of the capitol of the greatest government on the Earth—which in turn paid fealty to a government not of this Earth.

A minute passed in the silence of the room.

"Did you need me for something, sir?" Lepus finally offered, in his most humble voice. The word "sir" came out sounding like "sah."

"No, you can go, Lepus. Just don't go too far."

Lepus grinned, like a crocodile sunning itself on a rock, and left.

GAVIN ROSS PLACED THE phone down in the cradle and considered the report he had just received. He was not a stupid man, and he had gathered his forces for too long to lose them on some frivolous goose chase now. MAJESTIC-12's misguided little brother Delta Green was off on another of its cowboy operations. But disrupting the illegal conspiracy could cause problems.

Such an undertaking would require a great deal of preparation and dedication. Now was not the time. He had already made headway—startling progress, really—into the workings of the conspiracy. He had an inside view of the game. Despite this, he had not expected what he read in the report he just received. Not a hint of it had leaked to him.

A shootout in suburban Philadelphia at three in the morning had claimed the lives of seven people, including two state troopers, an off-duty police officer and one man tagged from Bostick's project

GARNET file searches as a once-active member of Delta Green. In early 1997, GARNET had done a compilation and sweep of all pre-1970 military files in the United States that were marked with a small green delta stamp, once the call-sign of Delta Green. Since then, Ross had received more than twelve alerts on these personnel. They had a habit of turning up dead in shootouts and under more bizarre circumstances. He also had other resources to peruse from time to time.

The room where the shootout took place was registered to a credit card which was nothing more than a blank, owned by a Mr. Olive, described by the hotel clerk as a large man in his mid-fifties. A car rented by Mr. Olive was found abandoned at Philadelphia International Airport that same day, along with an assortment of credit cards, identification cards and papers made out to Mr. Forest Olive.

Ross wondered what it could all mean. There was an agenda at work here. He was sure the message had been communicated for a specific reason, in the hope of a specific outcome, but whose reason? Kroft's? Lepus'? Delta Green's?

And for what outcome?

Ross picked up the phone and dialed an elaborate number, waited for the tone, verified his voice through the voiceprint system and waited. The line connected after a brief pause.

Had they known his identity, almost everyone in Delta Green would have been shocked to hear him say:

"B-Cell? This is Agent Adam. What the hell is going on in Philadelphia?"

Startling headway had been made, indeed.

The Alamo

Class One paranormal event: Days Inn, 2221 Highway 76, Philadelphia, Pennsylvania. 39.93 N/75.18 W latitude/longitude. Approximately 96 miles from Mount Weather, Virginia: Friday, February 2, 2001, 2:25 A.M. EST.

THE KNOCKING AT THE door was so sudden and unexpected that both men were immediately startled from sleep. There was no middle ground, no drowsiness; they had discarded such novelties through biological necessity long ago. Both went from dead asleep to wide-awake in less than a second. The room was dark except for the glowing dial of Poe's watch on the end table between their two beds and the night sky above the curtains in the window. They had learned in Groversville that splitting the team up—even in separate rooms in the same hotel—was an unnecessary risk. It was all about controlled movement, careful forethought, and luck.

Luck was what allowed learning to occur; and luck never gave out free second chances.

McRay reached over to switch on the light, but even in the dark he saw the warning in the white glint of Poe's eyes. Poe retrieved his pistol from the end table and slowly cocked it. The big man was nothing more than a silhouette outlined in the light coming through the window.

McRay rolled out of bed and fumbled for his shoulder rig, piled on top of his half-open suitcase. He found the reassuring block of his pistol and readied it as well. He wore no shoes or pants, just old blue and white jockey shorts and his T-shirt.

"It's Edwards," a voice hissed beyond the door.

"Not good," Poe mouthed. *Duh,* McRay thought. He had seen the shadows as well. The only way out was through the front door or the front window.

But other shadows were milling in front of the window. With the shades drawn completely it was not possible to identify them, but shapes moved there—at least three men, backlit by the occasional headlights passing on Highway 76.

"Are you alone?" Poe asked, from his hunched vantage point behind the bed, muzzle pointed at the door.

"Ye—" the voice began but was cut short by the huge report of Poe's pistol. A smoking shell leapt onto the bed and glinted in the dim light. A hole the size of a silver dollar ripped through the door at head level and exploded outward. A gurgling, coughing sound could be heard from outside, followed by a high-pitched ringing whine which shook the air. The shadows disappeared from the window instantly. Below, in other rooms, McRay could hear startled, muffled exclamations. A phone began to ring somewhere.

"Sorry, Eddie," Poe said, mostly to himself, and placed his pistol on the bed. His hands slid under the box spring and came back out with the gun he had assembled the day before. It was a squat black submachine gun with what looked like a too-long barrel, an MP5/10SD with an integral suppressor. He glanced back at McRay and McRay nodded, wishing vainly that he had a bigger gun with more ammunition, with a higher rate of fire—or even better, that he had never come here at all, that he was someplace safer, like Auschwitz or inside the burning Waco compound. McRay crossed the room to a point behind the bureau near the door, holding his pistol like a fading hope. Outside, past the jagged hole in the door, was blue-black night sky.

Poe inserted a huge clip in the submachine gun and looped its strap over his shoulder.

The door blew inwards. Thousands of fragments swept the room, a deadly rain of shrapnel. Something whizzed past McRay's left ear and he had moment to recognize the ruined remains of the chain lock, embedded in the wall like a spent projectile, before shapes began to boil through the door.

They were human shapes but they were not human. Eddie Edwards led the way. A hole was drilled through his jaw to the back of his head like an apple that had been cored, but somehow he—it—was still alive. Its eyes rolled madly in their sockets and fixed on McRay. Edwards leapt for McRay like an ape, its feet barely touching the ground as it covered the distance between them. McRay heard a ripping sound that he realized were Edwards' pants as the thing cleared the bureau in one hop. The thing's hands were fixed in murderous claws and its ruined mouth twitched, spilling liquids and shattered teeth. McRay brought the pistol up to bear on Edwards but wasn't fast enough.

Poe was.

A stuttering, coughing machine-like sound filled the room. Edwards was ripped by bursts of gore in mid-flight as Poe strafed the wall with the submachine gun. All McRay could do was say a prayer for the people in the next room. Edwards' head popped in two gushing sprays of gore. His left arm was rendered into a paste of fragmented bones and pulped flesh. His chest shook twice, spitting gouts of blood all over the wall behind him. Edwards hit the bureau in a crash, smashing the already shattered mirror into a million more fragments. The body slid across the surface of the wood in a wet lump and knocked McRay to the ground. McRay felt the unexpectedly heavy weight of Edwards' body smash into his face with shocking force. His pistol went flying and struck the wall behind him. McRay and the ruined form of Edwards collapsed to the rug in a bloody heap.

Then Poe really began to open up on Edwards' colleagues, nothing more than a clot of humanoid shadows lit by the rectangle of the breached door.

The window exploded first, a sound so loud and so commanding that it drowned out the racket of the suppressed gunfire for a moment. McRay struggled to pull free of the corpse, shifting its weight to get out from under it. To escape. To help Poe escape. Grunts and shouting filled the room under the staccato submachine gun sounds. Whistling, popping, screams, the chink-chink of casings spilling to the soft rug. Throughout all this, the endless phut-phut-phut of the submachine gun, a soundtrack to match the carnage.

McRay realized with a sudden maddening fear that the corpse would not roll off him no matter how he struggled. The corpse was moving in its own fashion, shifting its weight to counter his attempts at escape. Something ropy and thin, wet like a snake dipped in warm Vaseline, crept up McRay's naked leg, searching for ingress, probing. The remains of Edwards' lower jaw shifted and shook. One fully functional hand shot out suddenly with terrible strength and snapped closed on McRay's right wrist. A mad urge to just let it happen, to just give in to the lunacy, settled on McRay's mind like an obscuring fog.

McRay screamed then for the first time. He had been too shocked to scream at first. Whatever pall had fallen on his mind in the struggle vanished instantly with the shriek.

The Edwards-thing began to churn and shake above him in a convulsive fit, spewing dark, bile-like liquids all over McRay and the wall, but its grip never faltered. Foam formed at the lip of its empty, stump-like neck and spilled over like a blood-red tide.

There was a stunning, teeth-rattling explosion, and McRay felt a lick of flame flash past his right side, searing his skin. The Edwards-thing let forth an inhuman guttural cough, reacting to the flame, and rolled off McRay into the corner next to the bureau, hissing through the hole in its neck, like a startled animal. Somewhere deep in McRay's mind a note was made: *It hates fire. It hates fire. It hates fire.* This thought looped and looped, blotting everything else out.

McRay was up, stumbling backwards toward the bathroom wall. He snatched his gun up in two tries and brought it around on the Edwards-thing—it had somehow recovered and begun slinking towards him, propelling itself with motile intestines and destroyed limbs. McRay's gun jumped twice. Two shots hit the remains of the thing's head squarely, reducing it to bloody chunks.

It has no head, it has no head, it has no head, his mind kept idiotically repeating, over and over. McRay emptied his pistol into the thing, laughing and screaming as explosions of gore rippled through it.

McRay leapt for the far side of his bed when the action indicated the magazine was empty, only vaguely aware of the forms locked in combat on the other side of the room. If there was no combat going on, he reasoned, it would mean Poe was already gone. McRay landed in the dark of the bed and fumbled with his suitcase as a burst of submachine gun fire rippled through the room. McRay's hands found the small black clips in the bag.

Despite the gunshot-dullness of all sounds, McRay somehow heard sirens in the distance.

McRay reloaded and leapt up. What he saw there froze him in his tracks.

The other things were not just people, he saw for the first time. They once had been, perhaps, but now they were something more than the limit of their corporeal forms. Their bodies had intertwined into a patchwork of limbs. Feet in mouths grown over with connective tissues, hands intertwined with hands scabbed over to become one rough limb. The three men looked like obscene acrobats, locked together in some fatal position, but they—it—moved with the lithe grace of a powerful animal. Poe stood before it, beneath it, like a disciple, gun upraised but empty. Poe's gun was empty and the thing was lunging across the bed at him.

McRay jumped and hit the other bed in one huge bounce, springing across the gap between the beds, straight over Poe's head, without any real idea of what he was doing. In mid-air he fired wildly into the thing and then connected with its face, one of its faces, trying in vain to hang on to his gun so it would not be lost in the collision. It was like hitting a brick wall, but a wall that was not fastened to the floor. The thing tumbled backwards off Poe's bed and onto the ledge of the shattered window, scuttling like a crab knocked onto its back, trying to recover. McRay rebounded off and spilled to the ground onto shards of shattered mirror, crashing down onto his shoulders and neck. His gun went flying into the dark. For a moment he faded out of consciousness; it felt like his mind was tossed up and out into the dark.

The fire alarm went off, followed rapidly by sprinklers. The room filled nearly instantly with a fine haze of freezing water and the flashing warning of emergency lights from outside. McRay sat up with some difficulty and was immediately pulled to his feet and before he could recover, roughly shoved by huge hands. He stumbled backwards in quick steps through the open bathroom door, all balance lost, and his calves connected with the porcelain of the bathtub. He crumpled into the tub, striking his head hard enough to taste blood. Suddenly a huge black weight fell on him. In the same moment that he realized it was Poe, a thunderous explosion shook everything in the room. From his limited vantage point, McRay saw the ceiling in the other room lit by red and orange flames.

Poe dragged McRay to his feet, wheezing. The two stumbled out into the ruin of the room. Of the things, only the Edwards creature still seemed to have some life in it. The jelly-like pile of broken limbs and organs trembled occasionally but otherwise seemed unable to move. The horribly intertwined creature was nothing more than a debris field of limbs lit by the emergency strobes from the window over that wasteland-like side of the room. Water rained down from the ceiling, extinguishing the flaming bed. The floor was scorched, and in one small area near where Poe's bed had been it was completely gone, leaving only a black rupture, an opening to the room below. The ruins of the end table were shattered near the window, thrown more than ten feet.

Poe was shouting at him. Although McRay, his ears ringing, could not hear him, he nodded.

Poe recovered his submachine gun, replaced its magazine, and then covered the door.

McRay yanked up some soaking pants and pulled on his shoes. He recovered his pistol from a puddle and slipped it in his pocket.

Poe shouted something else. McRay shook his head as he fumbled through his suitcase. He found the kit in which he carried everything of interest and snatched up his shoulder rig. As an afterthought he ripped the claim ticket off his luggage. It would give away his flight information.

McRay turned to see little puffs of orange plaster popping in the room on the upper windowsill, around the ceiling. It took him a moment to realize they were caused by gunfire. Gunfire coming from outside—from the ground.

Poe, who was crouched out of the range of fire of their assailants, took a small, ball-like object from his jacket pocket. He let the submachine gun hang from its strap and fiddled with the ball. He bowled it out the door where it skittered neatly beneath the guardrail and off the ledge to the parking lot below.

A coughing explosion erupted below, followed by screams.

Poe looked back. *Come on*, he mouthed.

The two men ran out into the siren-filled night.

Δ

Poe yanked McRay by the scruff of his shirt down the open-air walkway on the second level of the Days Inn. Below them two police officers lay on the ground, one madly scrambling for cover behind the burning cruiser, the other still with his hands over his ears. A hole the size of a basketball was punched through the roof of the car and all its windows had been blown out. McRay said a silent prayer for the cops, and saw other lights racing towards the scene from the darkness of Highway 76. The banister and the wall behind them suddenly erupted in puffs of gunfire. People were still shooting up at them from the ground. Then Poe grabbed him by the arm and yanked him back, hard.

The two men rushed up the walkway towards the stairs. As they ran, doors flew open and shut again just as rapidly, as each individual party caught sight of the fugitives. The sight of Poe and his MP5/10 was enough to make almost everyone turn and immediately run back into their rooms.

The sound that came from close behind them—the pop— seemed inconsequential to McRay, who had just survived an Alamo-type engagement without a scratch. He did his best to ignore it and run on. But his right leg folded suddenly and he spilled forward, smashing his nose on the metal guardrail of the walkway. The world was lost in a flash of white pain. Warmth filled his body and he could barely hear the screams or the stuttering reports of the submachine gun. He hit the ground in a heap and rolled over.

Shot, he thought. *Shot in the leg.*

Something smashed to the ground next to him, shaking the walkway. McRay looked over to see the dead face of a stranger, dressed in a T-shirt, eyes wide with shock. Most of the right side of his face had been ripped away in messy brown white chunks and a

.38 revolver was still clutched in his limp right hand. Its muzzle was smoking. Off-duty cop, McRay thought. A woman nearby screamed. He couldn't locate her.

Won't be open-casket, McRay thought idiotically.

Poe pulled McRay over his broad shoulders with a grunt, letting the submachine gun hang from his neck as easily as a tourist would carry a camera. Amazingly, the old man began to run with McRay in a fireman's carry. McRay's feet thumped along on the pillars next to the walkway like a stick dragged across a picket fence, and his leg screamed in agony. Cars screeched to a halt below them. Numb and dazed, McRay could hear the gunfire below, distant, ineffectual-sounding pops. Poe huffed and puffed as he took the stairs two at a time to the bottom. Only several dozen cops lay between them and freedom. Somehow, that didn't seem so bad. At least they were out of the room. At least the *things* were gone. He would gladly endure a prison sentence if he never had to see those things again. Five years? Forty? No problem.

Muffled demands were shouted at them through a spotty loudspeaker.

"Don't worry, kid, they'll never take us alive," the old man shouted. He laughed and pulled two more grenades from his windbreaker pockets, holding both of them in one palm like relaxation balls.

Although he was loath to do so, McRay passed out before he could see what happened next.

Friendlies

The conspiracy goes to ground: 351 Pine Street, Apt. 12, Society Hill, Philadelphia, Pennsylvania. 39.93 N/75.18 W latitude/longitude: Friday, February 2, 2001, 3:49 A.M. EST.

"KATH . . . um . . . someone's at the door for . . . um, you," Hysung said, rubbing her sleep-filled almond eyes in an almost comically childish gesture.

Kathleen Homberger sat up in the dark and returned the tired stare of her roommate. The trauma medicine textbook she had fallen asleep reading spilled off her chest as she leaned forward to check the time. The book slammed to the wood floor, shifted under its own weight and folded shut.

The old digital clock on the mantle read: 3:49 A.M. Crap.

"Right there," Kath coughed, and pulled on some jeans. Hysung disappeared back into her room.

Kath rushed to the front door after Hysung's door slammed shut, and fiddled with the peephole.

A huge man stood at the threshold. He wore a wet black windbreaker over his wide shoulders and his greying brown hair was disheveled. It looked wet, even frozen in some places. He looked as maybe fifty, maybe older; it was hard to tell from the lighting. His blue eyes stared implacably back into the peephole without apprehension. There was a small, black drab of what looked like dried blood on the left side of his nose, right on top of an old third-degree burn scar. His face was filthy with dirt. It was obvious Hysung had just heard the knock at the door and had not checked the peephole.

It was lucky that Hysung had no family in the country and no real friends beside herself. If the man on the stoop was part of the Group, as she thought he was, Kath was grateful for that fact but for little else. She was on shift in less than three hours. You don't call in sick as a resident. That was the first of the long and baroque list of rules of medicine.

Well, you had to start fucking up somewhere.

"Yes?" Kath asked through the door, her tired voice cracking.

"Kathleen Homberger?" The man's voice was a deep baritone. There was no fear in it.

"Yes?"

"We met at the Opera," he said, plainly enough.

Kath pulled the door open. The guy looked older up close, like some sort of optical illusion. There were subtle lines running on all points in his face, completing loops, curves and folds which were most predominant beneath the eyes. She guessed he was closer to sixty than fifty, but that he was in prime physical shape despite his age.

The man regarded her with a piercing stare. He seemed to be looking through her, like he was flipping through her memories, rating her on some internal system of merit. Kath suddenly felt very inexperienced.

"I'm Charlie. You the surgeon?" he asked, looking doubtful.

"Yeah, soon. I mean—I'm still a resident. I can help you," Kath stuttered.

"Well, I have an extra-credit assignment for you. But don't go looking for any gold stars. I left them at the crime scene."

CHARLIE DROVE AN OLD, beaten Mustang rich with body rot and primer paint. It may have once been red but now there was no way of telling. As Kath slipped around the car she could see two weapons on the floor of the passenger side. One was an enormous submachine gun, the other a small, efficient-looking pistol. There were stacks of clips next to the weapons. He was part of the Group, all right; the telltale signs were here. It was her first call since recruitment and she didn't want to screw it up. They needed her. She sucked it up and got in the car, trying to control the fear that fluttered in her stomach like prehistoric-sized butterflies.

Charlie slipped in next to her, barely squeezing into the car. Something uncomfortable and sticky was on her hand as she fastened her seat belt. Even in the dark she knew it was blood. There was no mistaking the smell. A small green troll doll on the dashboard smiled insanely at her with wide, luminous eyes. Somehow she got the feeling this was not Charlie's car.

"We have to go to UPenn Hospital," she said. Then, seeing the look on Charlie's face, she added, "For surgical gear." He simply nodded.

"Who's hit and where?" she asked as they began to drive.

"My partner, Cyrus. It's a clean hit in the left thigh—a .38, I think. No arteries, it's not bleeding enough for an artery hit, just a lot of meat taken off."

"You've done this before."

"Yeah, lots of times."

"Good. Take this left."

They drove on in silence to the hospital.

THE HOSPITAL OF THE University of Pennsylvania was a Level 1 trauma center, one of several in the Philadelphia metropolitan area. As they pulled up, Charlie slammed on the brakes before they could enter the emergency driveway loop. The look on his face was somewhere between distrust and fear.

Two police cars idled near the automatic doors, along with an ambulance with its doors thrown wide. All three had their lights flashing. As the Mustang screeched to a halt, one of the cops looked up from the double doors, squinting through the dark to see the car.

"Not here," Charlie said.

"I have to go in," she began. She tried another tack: "I need this equipment to help your partner."

"Go" was all he said, and she jumped out the car without looking back.

Inside, the hospital was a mess. The chief surgeon on the floor was poised over a police officer whose chest had been opened in the same manner as his shirt: ripped straight down the middle. The doctor was manually massaging the cop's heart with his left hand while looking at his gore-filled right hand for the time. Residents were scattered here and there treating people in various states of dress, most without adequate clothing for the weather. *Hotel fire,* she immediately thought, but changed her tune when she saw the cop in the corner with the obvious gunshot wound to the arm. He was grimacing as a resident stitched up a huge rupture in his upper bicep. The image was striking. Something serious had gone on. Something she had not experienced before, at least not at this volume.

Gunshot wounds.

Guns on the floor of the car.

She pushed the thought away.

Kath saw two of her friends covered in blood, struggling to suture closed an arterial rupture on a pale, unconscious old man. Two corpses on gurneys in the corner were concealed beneath sheets so red with blood they looked dyed. The police scanner near the charge desk was screaming orders in varying voices between random gouts of static.

Everything in her training screamed at her as she stood unnoticed in front of the scene of carnage, and she literally jumped at the strength of the feeling. She should be helping. She should be fixing the hurt. Like a fighter struggling to shake off a vicious jab she staggered away from the emergency room.

She slipped her key card into the slot of the storage room and entered quickly, deftly shutting the door behind her. She clicked on the light and grabbed a tackle box from the corner. She filled it with everything she would need, or at least everything she could get. She didn't have access to any controlled pharmaceuticals, but in a pinch ether would do. If her name came up on the security rolls, she could always claim to have been assisting here, during the incident.

She left as quickly as she came, unseen amid the chaos and confusion.

THEY DROVE FOR A long time, or so it seemed to Kath. South down 95, past Veterans Stadium toward the airport. On Airport Way they pulled into a gravel driveway that led to a fenced-in complex.

RENT-N-SAVE, the sign above the gate read. Someone had scrawled 'Half Life' in white spray-paint on the sign.

Charlie exited the car and punched a long series of numbers into the keypad on the gate. The lock buzzed and clicked open. PLEASE CLOSE THE GATE AFTER USE, a sign read next to it. After they drove in, Charlie did so.

The complex was filled with corrugated steel shacks, none larger than fifty by fifty feet, covering more than three acres of frozen land. They drove down the aisles to unit 133. Charlie stopped the car and hopped out. He clicked on an old red flashlight and walked to the shed.

Kath got out as well, carrying the tackle box in both hands.

Charlie slid the door open with one immense hand. Inside the cluttered shed, on a dusty cot, a gore-stained man weakly raised a pistol to greet them. The gun wavered like he couldn't focus on them. In nothing but a T-shirt and boxer shorts he looked like he had just swum in a pool of effluvia. Someone had tried to tie off the wounds, but the amount of blood was too much. Kath froze. Charlie raised both hands and stepped between her and the gun.

"Poe?" the man asked, but his voice was far away.

"Yeah, it's me, man, I got the Friendly." Apparently Charlie's real name was Poe. Or was that another alias? She decided it was best if she didn't try to figure such things out. It could be dangerous if she knew too much.

At the sound of Charlie's voice the man dropped his arm with a grunt, as if he had been holding it up for hours instead of seconds. His eyes closed. The gun struck the ground and slid away from his grasp.

Won't need the ether, Kath thought to herself.

"Help him," Charlie said, and Kath got to work.

Kill Them All

Lepus catches a whiff of the conspiracy: The "Country Club," outside Mount Weather, Virginia. 38.98 N/76.50 W latitude/longitude. Approximately 96 miles from Philadelphia, Pennsylvania: Saturday, February 3, 2001, 6:34 P.M. EST.

ADOLPH LEPUS HAD NO friends, only enemies of varying degrees. Few could match his devious mind and callous nature. Few could match him at anything, ever. It was not some false belief he had constructed to soothe a fragile ego (as far as he could tell, he no longer had one), it was just the way he saw it. The world was full of puppets. He was the man who pulled the strings. There was Lepus and then there was the rest of the world. No comparisons were possible or necessary. No one else mattered; how could he compare himself to them?

Sometimes he was almost sure he was the only person who was real at all.

Why else would he have gotten this far without being stopped? He had been getting away with it for as long as he could remember. His earliest memories of pulling the wool over the eyes of other "people" surrounded the animals he had killed as a kid. There had been a bout of pet disappearances around his family's farm, starting just as Lepus hit puberty, and no one noticed. Pets and farm animals. He could recall his first tottering steps as a . . . what? Psychopath? Madman? It was a state he thought akin to immortality. Everything in the world was an illusion. He was the only reality, his existence the only one that mattered. Strangling cats, breaking dog's heads open with sledgehammers, poisoning rabbits. It had become boring after a time, of course. Everything did. Tedious. But he had moved onward and upward. Kids. Old ladies. Enemy troops. Soon enough his talent had been noticed and he had found a paying job doing what he did best. Three hundred and eighty seven "people" had now met their end by his direct intervention. Many, many more by his indirect attentions, too many to count—not that he didn't find himself trying from time to time to settle on a number. As far as he was concerned, that number could never be high enough.

It was the only thing he looked forward to anymore. Each death was a confirmation of his supremacy.

"Sir," a Section DELTA agent drawled, and Lepus gave the man a short salute. Keep up appearances; never reveal your true intentions unless you mean to carry them through to the end.

Lepus retired to one of the recreation rooms in the endless complex of the Country Club. In it the NRO DELTA men monopolized the foosball table in the corner while several of Bostick's geeks watched a flat-screen television from the comfort of a tan couch, the same fucking color as everything else in the goddamn Country Club. His mind was lost in convoluted loops of intrigue, considering Ross' and Kroft's latest cat's-paw, looking at it from all the angles. He knew more about what they were doing than they thought he did, and he was prepared at any minute to make a play for the side he believed would win their quiet little war. Or maybe just let them duke it out in the dim hope that they would kill each other. Stranger things had happened. Or if he simply—

Lepus froze.

On the television, a hazy, black-and-white photograph of two men in a convenience store was displayed on CNN. PHILADELPHIA SHOOTINGS, the caption read.

"One of the worst shootouts in Pennsylvania history occurred late last night in suburban Philadelphia, claiming the lives of three state troopers and five innocent bystanders. Today the biggest manhunt in state history has begun to bring those perpetrators to justice. The police are looking for these two men in connection with the crime—"

Lepus knew the two men in the picture. One was very fucking well known to him, indeed. Memories of Vietnam swam into his mind—dangerously weak memories. Fear, blind panic, things he didn't believe himself capable of feeling anymore. Or at the very least hoped he was no longer capable of feeling. Weakness was not an option in his line of work. He had jettisoned that and lesser emotions into some inner chasm some time ago and they had sunk silently into his black depths without a fuss. But they seemed restored to their former power now as he watched the television. They suddenly sprouted from the blackness of his mind like derelict artifacts of a dead civilization. He had been foolish, mistaking the blackness within him for a void. The things he had discarded remained behind, submerged in the muck, waiting for moments like this to emerge.

His mouth worked but nothing came out.

Twice he had gone to the brink. Twice he had seen the way things really were. But what had happened in both situations he could not clearly recall. The details of both events were gone, along with, he had thought, the weakness. But now, didn't it feel close to how it used to be? It did.

The memories were flat and unresponsive. He would mull over his limited recollections sometimes, like a man picking at a healing cut. Sometimes something would come out.

He still dreamed of Cambodia, of Puerto Rico, when some sick, mutated version of normal sleep spat out things his waking mind could not handle. In his dreams he was still human. But only there. Only in his dreams was he still vulnerable—until now.

A reporter came on the television, reporting live from one of the worst shootouts in Pennsylvania history, looking gleeful and fulfilled, like a leech that had found a rich host on which to feed. The news repeated again and again. The photo was taken during a credit card purchase made by one of the suspects, a Mr. Olive, considered an alias by the authorities. His accomplice's name was unknown.

No fucking shit. Really, an alias? You think?

Lepus was not surprised that the men, probably just the two of them, had decimated those state troopers. How many civs had they gotten, seven? The cops had gotten off lucky. Poe knew his trade. Poe was the trigger, the connection, the reason Lepus felt the way he did. Poe was the embodiment of everything human and weak waiting within Lepus. Poe was the reason.

They had butted heads only once after the war, after OBSIDIAN. Lepus had thought the clusterfuck at Groversville had marked the end of Poe and the other guy in the picture, Mc-something. The whole town had shriveled up and died from the fast virus, but Poe had survived, somehow. Somehow the man was still around. Somehow.

"Oh Poe, you fuck," he whispered. "I'll kill you. I'll kill you all."

The NRO DELTA men at the foosball table stood staring at him, the game long forgotten, waiting for directions, recognizing his mood shift. Bostick's geeks were frozen with fear on the couch, trying desperately not to draw attention to themselves. Lepus' temper was well known within the MAJESTIC community. Hell, it was even encouraged.

"Captain," Lepus barked.

"Sir," the NRO DELTA man shouted, snapping a salute.

"Get the choppers ready."

Lepus didn't realize he had pulled his pistol from his holster until the television in front of him exploded in a flash of smoke and shattered plastic. He looked down at the geeks cowering on the couch.

"I fuckin' hate Ted Turner," he whispered, and flashed them a wide, gold-toothed, huckster's smile.

Need to Know

Official intervention in the disappearance of Robert M. Lumsden: New Brunswick, New Jersey. 40.48 N/74.46 W latitude/longitude. Approximately 54 miles from Philadelphia, Pennsylvania: Wednesday, February 7, 2001, 10:12 A.M. EST.

CHARLIE BOSTICK HATED FIELD ops, so he was pleased that he rarely had time to do them. Unfortunately the connection he discovered between the death of Timothy Moriarity and the disappearance of Robert Lumsden was too big to be ignored. So he made the time.

At first glance the two men seemed totally unconnected, separated by an entire continent and completely different lines of work. But he had verified it in a side trip to Philly: The two men had attended the same high school in Philadelphia and had graduated in the same class, in 1989. It was more than likely they had known each other. It was a small school.

Coincidences that big did not happen.

In addition, both incidents—the seeming resurrection of Michael Lumsden (Bob Lumsden's little brother!) and the death of Timothy Moriarity had occurred after Bob Lumsden had disappeared under mysterious circumstances. The Michael Lumsden case, which had just broken over the national news like a tidal wave, seemed more important to cover up—but Bostick's instincts told him the source was here, in New Brunswick, with the disappearance of the kid's older brother. He would cover up the kid later, if that were necessary, or even possible. Somehow, it didn't seem that important right now. He would think of something; right now, his mind was on other matters.

It seemed plain to him that it all had begun in New Brunswick.

If the police were correct in their conclusion that Bob Lumsden disappeared sometime on the evening of the twenty-second of January, then it seemed a clear chain of events had occurred from that point onward. On the twenty-fourth his dead little brother appears in his parent's house, none the worse for wear. On the twenty-sixth his schoolmate Timothy Moriarity is killed in a novel manner, and the scene of the crime is . . . tampered with. On the thirty-first Moriarity's corpse gets up and goes for a walk. BLUE FLY was sure that last part was evidence of an alien parasite, a threat that MAJESTIC was well acquainted with from a past operation. Bostick was not convinced.

It seemed clear enough to him that they were dealing with another David Nells-type incident. But the Steering Committee would be hard to convince without cold, hard facts, and it was hard to find cold, hard facts when you were dealing with the paranormal. Add to that the fact that David Nells was a nightmare that no one at MAJESTIC was ready to consider again so soon, and Bostick's work was cut out for him.

Nells had appeared and gunked up the works several months before, trashing the Puerto Rico OUTLOOK facility—right after they had lost the Maryland facility to a Delta Green raid—and killing dozens of valuable personnel with one of his little miracles. The guy could do things, amazing things. But despite extensive examinations by Yrjo and his OUTLOOK goons before all hell broke loose, no one knew why or how. And no one knew where he was now. Just like Bob Lumsden.

What about *that* coincidence?

So Bostick, despite all his reservations, was out in the field, decked out in an expensive but ill-fitting suit. Earlier he had posed as an FBI agent, flanked by two NRO DELTA goons in similar disguises. They muscled in (or rather his bodyguards had muscled in, and he had followed) and demanded the files on the Bob Lumsden case from the local police. It was kind of cool, really. Who else got to pretend to be an FBI agent and got real FBI credentials for their little farce? No one he could name—well, no one outside of MAJESTIC. It was hard not to slip into the mode of all the TV shows he had watched so religiously growing up.

Just the facts.

He had saved so many fumbles for the team that MAJESTIC no longer kept him on the short leash reserved for other flight risks—and other flight risks consisted of almost everyone except the members of the Steering Committee themselves. He could shake off the confines of MAJESTIC from time to time at his own whim, as long as he did his job—or so it seemed. He supposed the two NRO DELTA flunkies with him could count as some insurance for the home team. But the Steering Committee had mellowed on his comings and goings, no doubt due to his amazing work in retroactively explaining away apparently unexplainable events. Dr. Yrjo was granted similar excesses, he knew. It felt . . . good that he was accorded such respect. It was nice to be appreciated for one's work. Still, it wouldn't take much for the whole charade that MAJESTIC had laboriously constructed since 1947 to disintegrate. And when MAJESTIC went, everything went—himself, the world, the whole ball of wax, everything.

And the pressure just kept building.

The police were not very happy about turning over the files on Lumsden's disappearance, but they had complied. The project that Lumsden was working on was federally funded, after all—at least, that's how it looked in the records by the time Bostick demanded the files—and Lumsden was a missing person. MAJESTIC descended on the New Brunswick area with casual efficiency, snatching files and gathering facts. They were still in Stage One. Look and learn.

Stage Two—if there was a Stage Two—was where Bostick would return to the Country Club and take a breather. He handled the file cleanup for those rare times Stage Two came into play. He knew all about Stage Two. Though he was never there and he only received bland reports afterward, he could very plainly see what a Stage Two did. You could spot a Stage Two from the gaps, the missing people. The lone suicides. The carjackings in broad daylight. The dead families with no relatives and no funerals.

He was forever filling in the gaps that drew questions. He answered the questions. Did it matter if the answers were lies?

What could he do? If a Stage Two was necessary, he'd be eating Häagen-Dazs and watching *Party of Five* when the real knuckle draggers showed up. Later he would put all the pieces together again with a little help from OUTLOOK—but it rarely came to that anymore. What could he really do?

It was best not to think of the people who had once filled those gaps. Bostick shrugged it off and considered the more immediate problems at hand.

Lumsden had been working on some strange stuff at Rutgers. Vincent Garrity, the leader of the project, could not be located, and neither could the prototype of the device that Lumsden had been working on. Bostick had learned enough about the project to scare him shitless. The Passive State Brain Monitor and Display sounded like seriously dangerous shit. If Yrjo and the boys had cooked one up (and Bostick was nearly certain they'd be kicking themselves that they had not), he would not have blinked twice. It sounded like one of the OUTLOOK brain drain's little projects. It wasn't hard to believe in psychic phenomena when you were able to review tapes of a guy making another guy explode with just the power of his mind. It wasn't a long stretch at all.

The PSBMD looked like a giant step in a bad direction. In a nutshell, the device scanned the brain state of a subject and displayed a color—beginning at red and ending at violet, cycling through the spectrum—on a screen that the subject watched. The goal was to shift the color to violet by consciously altering brain state, each color representing a calmer, more controlled state of mind. The problem was that strange things began happening to some subjects in the deeper states of consciousness. Things that weren't supposed to be possible. What notes Bostick was able to come across (and there were startlingly few) indicated that by the time a subject achieved the green level in the device, which was usually in less than a week, they could control autonomic functions—heartbeat and respiration. Basically the device was a way to mass-produce Yogis and other crazy mentalist gurus in a matter of days instead of a matter of years, with no special training required.

Every branch of the United States military would want it. If it did even more than just produce instant Yogis—and Bostick had the feeling it did—every individual within those branches would want it for themselves. If it did what Bostick thought it did—if it produced superhumans like Nells, who rained havoc on the OUTLOOK Group sixteen months before—every member of the Steering Committee would turn on every other member. If this was brought to their attention, MAJESTIC would disintegrate at speed, spewing secrets, corpses and intelligence that common humanity should never know. Who would come out on top of a war like that? Kroft? Ross? Lepus?

Bostick shivered. He would never let that happen.

The question was, to whom should he spill these little breakthroughs of his? As far as the committee knew, he was checking up on the Michael Lumsden case. He had informed no one of the significance of his discoveries—yet. More to the point, should he inform anyone? What if he was wrong? Somehow, despite the lack of evidence, he was pretty sure of himself. He couldn't shake the feeling that he was dead on the money, no matter how hard he tried.

What if he found the device himself? The NRO DELTA goons knew almost nothing about the case, and he had his doubts that they would understand the significance of the device even if they tried. He could probably step into it and use it and they wouldn't have a clue what the hell he was up to. As usual, he was the center, the convergence point for dozens of different events that only he could correlate and understand; only he had developed the eye necessary to pick them out of the background noise of the "real world." Who else could connect them?

Bostick laid back and turned on the television of the lavish hotel room he had been secreted in. On the screen Luke Perry scrunched his eyebrows down like caterpillars trained to perform synchronized acrobatics.

90210.

Cool.

Reunion, Class of '69

Lepus follows the trail: Days Inn, 2221 Highway 76, Philadelphia, Pennsylvania. 39.93 N/75.18 W latitude/longitude. Approximately 54 miles from New Brunswick, New Jersey: Sunday, February 4, 2001, 3:44 P.M. EST.

ADOLPH LEPUS SPAT INTO the ashes and considered the ruins of room 311. Poe had been here, all right. Every piece of furniture in the room was either shattered by an explosion or so pock-marked with submachine gun bullet holes that it was completely destroyed. Nothing, not even the floor beneath the scorched rug, was left intact. The window was blown out onto the walkway. A mirror had exploded on the mantle and was spread about the singed rug in a million glittering pieces. The bureau on which the mirror once sat was a wet hunk of shattered wood, all splintered edges and black soot. It looked like someone had stuffed it full of black powder, lit the fuse and stepped back to enjoy the show.

The wall next to the bureau was studded with over forty black bullet holes—just that one wall. Every other area in the room was also pierced dozens of times. An end table had been thrown against a wall so hard that no single piece was more than six inches long. The front door had blown inward and a chain lock from that door had been found embedded in the wall eight feet away.

One hundred and fifteen 10mm rounds were recovered at the scene by the police, including four from two of their own men—the general consensus was that there were more rounds laying about, waiting to be found. One had been located over a quarter mile away in a tree across the highway, reported by a person standing at the bus-stop nearby when it hit. An MP5/10SD in full automatic mode was the main culprit. Silenced, suppressed. Poe had changed nothing about his modus operandi except to upgrade his weaponry. The last time they had clashed, the old man had been humping it with an MP5 in the usual 9mm; Lepus knew because that time, they had pulled slugs from two of his men's heads.

Poe had been using anti-personnel grenades. He didn't need a report in the field to know they were M61's, Vietnam vintage. How could he forget? It was how Lepus had lost his teeth.

A clear picture of Poe, sweaty and crazed, smiling a madman's smile. A feeling of helplessness, the taste of metal in his mouth.

"You say nothing, Lepus. You say nothing. You say nothing or the birds will be picking you out of the grass for weeks."

He hadn't put away his grunt hat, after all these years. Poe *still* tossed grenades around casually, like it was an everyday thing. For Poe it was an everyday thing; for the cops, it was a different matter. The cops never stood a chance. They were lucky Poe wasn't after them specifically. Of course, the cops felt differently. They were sure he was some sort of ex-con or militia fanatic with a grudge against law enforcement. They had no way of knowing that Poe just wanted out and they were in his way.

Reports varied, but it was apparent his partner (McMillan or something) was hit during the skirmish. A cop who had been staying at the hotel, and who was found in his underwear with his brains all over the wall, had gotten one round off from a .38 before Mr. 10mm said hello and goodbye. Lepus would put better than even money that the shot had touched not Poe but his partner. The cops—those who were brave enough to raise their heads after the exchange began—reported seeing the big guy running with the little guy thrown over his shoulder in a fireman's carry, all the while firing at them with his MP5/10SD in one hand. Four other cops were hit during the three-minute duel. Two of them on the ground turned up not breathing at the end of it.

No one had yet identified the body parts found in the room

yet, for the main reason that those body parts were short one vital ingredient that usually led to a positive identification—a whole body. Various limbs were spread about the burned floor near the shattered window, scattered like the afterthought of some insane butcher who used high explosives to get the choicest cuts. No full limb had been found yet which could yield any clues to identity. Teeth were scattered all over like party favors. One almost-complete torso with an arm still intact (but without a head) was found, and was the only part of the remains in the room to be identified. The name of the deceased was Detective Edward Lawrence Edwards. Age 53. Dead cop number three.

But there was a difference with Edwards.

Lepus had glanced at that name more than once—it struck a chord in the depths of his mind. Corporal Edwards had aged a bit in his police file photo, but otherwise he looked like the same smartass he had been in Cambodia in 1969.

What did you do, Lepus? Get crotch rot fucking a dead NVA? Edwards' voice whispered in his mind. A voice that seemed not to be a part of him anymore. Like it was something from the outside that had come in and settled down to roost. A ghost, a demon; whatever. Lepus shook it off.

It was a regular fucking reunion here at the fucking Days Inn. Delta Green class of 1969. Welcome, graduates of Operation OBSIDIAN. As far as Lepus knew there were only five of them left, now—four, counting Edwards' torso as proof that he would not make it back next year to enjoy the festivities. But with Delta Green, you never knew for sure. . . .

One of the other graduates—you could probably call him the valedictorian—was in a loony bin in California. Tipler was his name. The guy had smoked eight people in a church in 1971 with a shotgun, shouting about things from outer space. OBSIDIAN did shit like that to you. You went nuts quietly or you went nuts loudly. One thing was sure, though: You went nuts.

Or you took the other route and flushed it all away. But was that any different from losing it quietly, after all?

With Edwards gone, that left just Poe and Lepus, Tipler and Waverly. Waverly was an Army fuck riding a desk in Washington. He looked normal enough on the outside, but Lepus was sure OBSIDIAN had touched him as well. NRO DELTA kept a quiet eye on him, just in case.

In Lepus' mind, a hit list was forming. He would have to clean house. But Poe was his priority; the other losers could wait. Lepus was almost sure the others would welcome death, after what they had all seen.

White silk and black sky.

The temple.

Something black and alive and bigger than the sky rising from flames and smoke—building itself, forming itself.

Men screaming.

Machine guns chattering like jungle insects.

He had covered it up, of course, even from himself. He had kept it from his waking mind. Nothing he recalled was clear enough to be labeled absolutely real. And wasn't that what going crazy was really about?

Lepus' unconscious smile faded from his face. He stepped further into the room and shook off the feeling. It was beneath him, the fear. The feelings.

But they did not go as easily as they once did.

Poe had been careful. His rental car was found ditched near the airport, littered with AB-Negative blood and phony credit cards. Phone records of the room showed a bunch of calling-card calls that were rerouted through the Cayman Islands and could not be traced further. Lepus was sure the card number was long gone, but MAJESTIC was checking it anyway. Neither of the men had used his real name and it seemed they had gotten away clean. The only pictures the authorities had of Poe and his partner were from a time-coded Circle K camera from the night before the bloodbath. The men had effectively vanished. It didn't really matter. Lepus knew who they were.

He could tell they were still nearby. Wounded animals always went to ground; all you had to do was find their burrow. And wasn't Lepus an expert at killing animals? Hadn't it been his overriding passion as a youth? Couldn't he track like a hound dog and kill like a grizzly?

You bet your fur he could.

Lepus' smile returned to his face slowly as he dreamily stared at the ruins of the room. It was a shame he hadn't been there to watch the destruction unfold. It was always unfortunate to miss the performance of a master. Truth be told, if he had been there, he wasn't at all sure which side he would have rooted for.

A Rendezvous

Class One paranormal event: Wellington Estates, Snohomish, Washington. 47.61 N/122.34 W latitude/longitude. Approximately 2,374 miles from Philadelphia, Pennsylvania: Friday, Sunday 4, 2001, 10:39 P.M. PST.

COLONEL ROBERT COFFEY CONSIDERED the uninhabited and incomplete model homes of the Wellington Estates through infrared goggles and felt something stir in his chest like the herald of approaching doom. Lit in red, a single human-sized form was visible through the wall of the supposedly empty building a hundred yards away. It slunk down into the basement and out of sight, the cold concrete obscuring its heat signature.

I have a rendezvous with Death at some disputed barricade, Coffey thought to himself, and waved a single black-gloved hand in two quick sweeps toward the building. Forty men rushed forward from the underbrush like shadows come to life.

Armed to the teeth, helmeted, anonymous and deadly, the men were the best. Compared to them, NRO DELTA was a goon squad, a place low-level Green Beret gorillas went to roost when they finally failed their psych evaluations. The team that Coffey commanded, BLUE FLY, was the elite. Its people were the best of the best. They and they alone had overcome dozens of alien threats. They had eliminated more than forty unknown species of creatures, threats that had found their ways to Earth for various reasons, none of them good. The men of BLUE FLY had toiled and lost their lives and gone on in complete secrecy, without thanks or reward, for the past twenty years. They protected what they knew and loved, and ensured the containment of secrets only MAJESTIC could ever know. They were good men. They were his men.

He was their leader.

Coffey rushed forward, taking up the tip of a large triangular formation as it crossed the dead space of the open field. Camaraderie. Faith. Freedom. He could feel all the years of training, all the lessons learned in battle, swell in him. The line of men enfolded the structure easily, wrapping it in a picket line of silent commandos.

I have a rendezvous with Death on some scarred slope of battered hill, Coffey thought. In his mind the words played out in the voice of his grandfather. He could see him even now—a man dead forty years, a frail man in a steel folding chair reading from a book of poems. A man who had walked through the death and carnage of two world wars untouched. A man who had died with a shit-bag on his hip in an old-age home. Coffey had marked the old man's words before he was gone. Coffey had learned that death was something to be sought. If you did not seek it, it could be a long, long time coming. Sometimes too much time was not a good thing. Sometimes old age was not a blessing.

Coffey was resolute. He would not die in some bed, eaten alive by time. He would meet death face on, and though he knew he would lose, there would be a victory in that loss. An honor in his final defiance of that magnificent and total power.

Everything—everything—died.

"Stand by, Five," Coffey ordered into the microphone at his collar. A light in the night sky winked once, a single white eye in the heavens, then it was gone. It was from a helicopter, completely silent and invisible.

"I've got you, Four," a Southern-accented voice responded in his headset.

Coffey and three of his men took up defensive positions at the back door of the model home.

Project GARNET personnel had noticed a link between four recent disappearances in the Seattle area since the alien's escape from the morgue on January 28th. Each disappearance had something to do with the Wellington Estates complex. The track houses were to be sold next December, when the construction was complete, but Coffey doubted that would ever occur. If what he thought was here was here, and had made a nest, it would all have to go, just to be safe. This place would look like the surface of the moon when he was done with it.

The disappearances were suggestive. One worker from the site had not shown up for work in more than four days and his apartment was found abandoned. A house painter who had been employed at the site was also gone, under similar circumstances. Two town zoning officials had gone missing together at the site, and the police had been alerted. MAJESTIC, lying in wait, stepped in. A flyover by MAJESTIC aircraft had located an anomalous heat source in one of the western units in the complex. As the crow flies, the building was less than eleven miles from the morgue. Between the two locales was mostly open wilderness.

As far as the local police knew, the case was now under federal jurisdiction. As usual, with the usual threats applied, cooperation was reluctant but inevitable and instant.

MAJESTIC suspected the Traveler species—that was the alien's classification from MAJESTIC's Project PLUTO. The creature was tricky. It was a neural parasite that could control a host organism like a puppet. No sign of the typical Traveler spacecraft had been found, despite numerous flyovers and satellite photographs of the area, but video footage from the morgue attack showed what seemed to be very clear evidence of a Traveler.

Coffey had dealt with this type of alien twice before, once in Arizona in 1996 and once in Montana later that year. Four men had been lost in the first operation, one of the worst fiascos BLUE FLY had ever suffered. Mistakes like that operation would never be made again.

If the creature were allowed to breed, there was no knowing how far it could get. It was Coffey's job to see it never got to that point. Coffey always did his job.

Whenever possible he did it personally, just to be sure. It was frowned upon, of course. The higher-ups had their cat's paws and shadow-plays to get him behind a desk, and the officers underneath him often were left weak-willed and looking to him too much. He could see that, he wasn't stupid. But the men loved him—even the ones he trampled over with his commands—and there was nothing like being in the field.

All eyes were on him. The house was surrounded. The perimeter was secure. Brief, concise reports flowed to him through the complex radio protocol, up the chain of command like dominoes spilling over in precise, carefully planned reactions, painting patterns. The windows of the basement had been sealed in some manner, unlike the other buildings. No heat targets were observable on the upper two stories. Front window right—clear. Front window left—clear.

"The basement," Coffey murmured. The lead man blew the door open with a lock-cutter shot from a matte-black automatic shotgun and his team moved in rapidly, rushing up the stairs and into the house. Reports of the team pouring in the front door told the tale. No targets, no cover, no threat visible. The house was completely empty of furniture.

Coffey followed Anders, the lead man, through the complex layout of the building towards the basement staircase. They had studied the floor plans of the five different types of houses offered at the estates. They had the plans memorized like rote lessons, now, hard-written into each man's memory. A wrong turn or misstep could cost a second in disorientation and the whole team its collective life.

BLUE FLY did not make those kinds of mistakes.

Through the goggles the door to the basement was an orange

blur. A consistent heat source was lighting the area below at a constant, sauna-like level. Thermal imagers would be useless.

I've a rendezvous with Death at midnight in some flaming town, Coffey thought.

"Goggles," Coffey murmured and the four men flipped up the tiny sight amplification rigs that rode the lips of their helmets, exposing their eyes.

Three expectant pairs of eyes stared back at him, sweaty and wide with excitement. The job was a natural high, a near-perfect rush, next to which any other activity was boring. The real world was bland and without color; only during an op did the world seem to be rendered with Technicolor vividness. Coffey would never willingly surrender his field command. If he fulfilled his wish and met death well, he would never have to. Anders placed a gentle hand on the doorknob. He twisted the silvery fixture one way and then the other. The door was locked from the inside.

Anders blew the door. The round punched the entire lock out in a ragged black hole, and he immediately swung the short shotgun around on its strap, bringing up his submachine gun in one swift move. A horrible, rich smell wafted out, overtaking the smell of gunpowder in a wave—a smell like a slaughterhouse floor left to bake in some impossible, endless summer sun for a year. The solid oak door, hinged outward, suddenly exploded open, swept wide by a giant unseen force. It struck Anders squarely in the head and threw him to the ground. His submachine gun slid across the hardwood floor to the far white wall, where it rebounded off into the dark like a misshapen hockey puck. Anders lay unconscious or dead on the floor, his super-fiberglass helmet split neatly into four sections, as if it were as fragile as an egg.

"Bandit's in the basement!" Coffey shouted, and since his field of fire was apparently clear of friendlies he opened up with his MP5.

Responses came from all members in the three units of his team not present with him at the door. Help was on the way. Men thumped down from upstairs to rush to his aid.

The submachine gun hopped in his hands like a thing alive and he clenched his teeth and tried to hold on to the rattling contraption as best he could. The blackness of the stairwell was lit in stark white flashes like a strobe light as each round leapt from the barrel. Coffey looked down the stairs in those brief moments of light and saw madness looking back at him with a hundred lidless eyes.

A pink wall of flesh, filling the whole stairwell—and as far as Coffey could tell, the whole basement—was squeezed into the narrow diagonal passage like Silly Putty pushed into a jar, human-like flesh in random splotches of anatomy. Bulbous eyes, hundreds of them, lidless and green and white, stared up at him with an obvious, reactive intellect, and a hundred ropy limbs reached for him like boneless arms. The structure of the thing had no rhyme or reason. A limb was here, an eye there, sometimes both in the same place. It moved with a terrible fluidity, suggesting the extreme mobility of octopi or amebas. Roiling limbs snaked out, searching for prey.

Tiny black dots appeared in the mass of the beast as Coffey fired, little black pinholes in the sickly pink skin that closed as soon as they appeared, leaving behind not even the slightest trace of a wound. Punctured eyes spewed forth a yeasty yellow liquid that when shaken off by movement revealed a new and unharmed eye, none the worse for wear.

The wrinkled skin of the creatures' leading edge stretched closer to him, reacting to the bullets, curling in on itself and twisting. It was not until the rock-hard tentacle closed around his ankle that Coffey realized that the thing was opening a huge, uneven maw filled with foot-long serrated teeth to greet him.

Other men had joined him at the edge of the doorway and were firing wildly into the hole—but by then, Coffey was unceremoniously yanked off his feet by the ropy limb. The BLUE FLY members ceased firing instantly, so they would not hit their commander as he dropped down two steps toward the giant gaping mouth. His feet, pointing down, were now less than seven feet from the thing.

O'Donnell leapt forward and caught Coffey in a strong palm-to-palm grasp. Behind him, Coffey could see another BLUE FLY man struggling to hang on to O'Donnell, to give him an anchor. The entire mass of the three men shifted as the thing below gave a tug on Coffey's boot. Tendons popped in his leg like rubber bands snapping under a heavy weight. The pain was sick and sweet and real. Another tremendous limb fell roughly on Coffey's back, but slid off before it could find a grip.

"Your other hand, sir!" O'Donnell shouted. It was only then that Coffey noticed the high-pitched, bone-shaking notes of music that rose and fell like a tide of sound from the basement. It sounded like some immense wind instrument made to play by the gusts of a hurricane. It was huge. It was titanic. Windows shattered one after the other as the noise cycled up and down. Pipes. Giant pipes, Coffey thought, as the pain in his leg grew and he shifted his other hand toward O'Donnell.

Then he knew. As sure as he knew his name. This was it. This was his place. His time. His free hand grabbed onto the plank of the unfinished step instead of finding O'Donnell's other hand. The music seemed to recede like a fading dream.

"Execute Yankee protocol," he hissed through clenched teeth over the comnet. He heard all three units accept his report, chattering madly in his ear, all reserve gone from their voices. Men opened doors and fled into the night. Anywhere but within one hundred yards of the target. O'Donnell still clutched his other hand, defiantly refusing his order. The man behind him struggled somberly, refusing to give in. To give up.

Coffey's boot popped clean off his foot on the third yank, taking a chunk of skin with it and snapping several bones in process. He clenched his teeth and released his grip on O'Donnell's hand. His hand slid down two steps and wrapped numbly around the plank there. The thing pulled lazily at his other leg, testing.

His grip held, for the moment.

A dozen or more smaller ropy limbs fell on his legs, trying to grasp him as he wrapped one elbow around the plank and hung on for life. O'Donnell dodged a probing limb which swept near the feet of the men at the lip of the door.

Coffey looked up into the blue, scared eyes of O'Donnell and locked there.

"I gave you an order, son," he mouthed. His words were lost in the crescendo of sound, but the meaning was clear.

Shaken, O'Donnell turned and ran and the second man followed. Two shadows rushed by a second later with a third form held between them, two men carrying the unconscious or dead Anders in a rushing, shambling gait. A wave of pride swept through Coffey as he saw his men act as he would act, as they did what he would do.

Reports started to file in, various voices of his four units chiming in over the comnet.

"Safe distance," they reported, one after the other. Coffey counted each report, waiting for thirty-eight as the creature groped for purchase. Waiting for death to take him.

A tentacle the size of plumbing pipe wrapped around his chest and noosed tight, cutting off his breath. The wood plank creaked as the beast tugged on him experimentally, like a tongue probing a piece of food lodged between teeth. The thing knew it had time to spare. It had time to savor. Or so it thought. Coffey had other plans.

He did not have a death wish—he had a mission. He didn't

know what this thing was—it sure as hell wasn't a Traveler—but that changed nothing. It was obviously alien and it was obviously a threat.

The mission wasn't complete, not yet.

Coffey saw spots before his eyes as number thirty-eight reported in. The tugging became more insistent and he could feel distant popping cracks ripple through his numb body as his armor shut like a vise around his ribcage. Ribs snapped like balsa wood as the plank on which his elbow was locked began to pull free of the staircase. The tentacle, searching for better purchase, shifted down his body to his abdomen and wrapped around it twice tightly. Coffey's chest felt like it was filled with broken glass as he inhaled. His breath came in and out of its own accord, trying to restore his oxygen, each lung screaming in agony as it expanded and contracted.

"Five, target my position," Coffey hissed through clenched teeth. The wood plank tore free with a squeaking crack.

"Copy that, targeting your position, Four," the distant Southern voice responded. "Colonel—" the voice began, and then fell silent. Training—training overcame all sentiment and good intentions. In the gulf of fear, there is only training.

"Good luck, sir."

Coffey scrambled as he slid down the stairs, still desperately clutching for an anchor. Somehow his hand found a hold of something, and he could feel his arm and abdomen stretching to their limits and beyond. The beast pulled him again and his shoulder popped audibly, like pistol shot. But beneath the noise of his shoulder cracking he only felt the sound.

The light that rose through the house then was clear and clean. A white light unlike any Coffey had ever seen. No one had ever seen such a light and lived to describe it. The pocket neutron weapon, with less than one ton yield, would decimate every living thing within eighty yards, erasing flesh and bone in a wisp, evaporating biological material, leaving only scorched husks of buildings behind. Coffey was glad the yard outside was not in bloom, that the plants outside were sleeping and winter-dead, and he marveled at the strange thought, and that he had time to think it. He would never see the spring.

When spring trips north again this year,

And I to my pledged word am true,

I shall not fail that rendezvous, Coffey thought, as the perfect cleansing light went into his eyes and through them.

Feints Within Feints

Lepus lays down his hand: Radisson Hotel, 15 Fulton Street, Philadelphia, Pennsylvania. 39.93 N/75.18 W latitude/longitude. Approximately 2,374 miles from Seattle, Washington: Monday, February 5, 2001, 4:06 A.M. EST.

THE PHONE WAS RINGING. Lepus snatched it up and sat up in bed. He had been sleeping uneasily, dreaming of things he could not recall clearly—and for that simple fact he was profoundly grateful. He was fully dressed in his usual black suit. He wiped the sleep from his eyes as he struggled to regain his edge. He looked like a corpse come back to life to critique its own funeral.

"Lepus," he spoke into the encrypted flip-phone.

"Get your ass back to the Country Club, we have a situation," Ross barked into the phone. Lepus' supposed boss was in rare form tonight.

Lepus glanced at the clock on the mantle and considered the options. Something catastrophic had happened. Most likely some ass-up involving BLUE FLY or ZEUS. Maybe the Greys had finally returned MAJESTIC's hundreds of unanswered communications or had snatched another base. Perhaps Ross had sensed Kroft finally moving in for the kill.

"What are you talking about?" Lepus said, pushing back his hair.

"Coffey's dead. Kroft has hit the ceiling. Get back here, now." Ross' voice was full of ire. Shit rolls downhill—the first rule of politics. Right now, by his calculations, Lepus was in the number three shit-slurping spot. But not for long.

He had considered his options, and had tried to stretch the time between his silent, stage-left exit from the Country Club and his final confrontation with those in command. Now his hand was forced.

He had things to do. He had people to kill and places to level, and he sure as hell didn't need Gavin "High and Mighty" Ross looking down his nose at him all the while. Or, worse yet, Ross putting the kibosh on his little reunion plans.

"You know what, Ross?" Lepus responded casually. "You are a Pure D asshole. You can take your command and stick it up your pinhole-sized ass. That is, if you can make it fit."

Silence on the line.

"This is no time for fucking jokes," Ross said as if this kind of insubordination was commonplace. "Get your team back here now." But Lepus could smell the panic. Ross was trying too hard to pretend nothing was wrong.

"Who's joking, you spineless freak? I don't need you anymore. I've got shit to do. Stop getting in my way."

"Lepus, you go AWOL again and Kroft won't protect you!" Ross hissed.

"Protect me? From who? You? Who you going to kill me with, old man? Coffey's gone. You got anyone else in Section DELTA you trust to side with you and not me? My own fucking men? Keep dreaming! How about in the recently widowed BLUE FLY?"

More silence on the line.

Ross was checking his calculations, suddenly unsure of his own part in the equation. The men of NRO DELTA worshipped Lepus in the way the SS had revered Hitler. Lepus was the epitome of the heartless killer, the archetype of the government mechanic—but it went beyond that. He added a level of art to casual destruction that only those socially dysfunctional people at NRO DELTA could admire. He was the Michelangelo of death. NRO DELTA would never turn on him consciously, although some would refuse to turn against MAJESTIC as well. Those few who would remain loyal to MAJESTIC would be of no use to Ross. And without leadership, BLUE

FLY could never stand up to a confrontation with NRO DELTA under Lepus.

"Besides, shithead, I took out some insurance," Lepus whispered, stretching the comment out, savoring the discomfort he could sense on the other end of the line.

"What do you mean, Lepus?" Ross's voice cracked with fear despite his impeccable phone etiquette, and Lepus could see him at his desk, a giant man hunched and broken and scared. Nothing more than a kid playing at being a mover and shaker. Ross, to Lepus' knowledge, had never killed a man; he had never even leveled a gun at one. He was a chump, and so was Kroft. The entire Steering Committee could go to hell. They were not hands-on. They did not know what it was like to cleanse the world.

They were not even real.

"Guess who's guarding your facilities, and your VIPs. Oh, and by the by, be sure to let Kroft know I've defected. That way, after you're dead for letting me get away with it, maybe I can come back get your job for being so clever. Movin' on up! To the East Side!" Lepus laughed and lay back on the immaculately-made bed. His entire face seemed split open sideways by his smile. The three gold caps on his teeth glinted in the dim light.

Ross hung up on him. The old man was probably scared out of his mind, trying to muster untenable forces through a dozen frantic phone calls. Trying to locate Bostick before NRO DELTA could spirit him off. Trying to keep this betrayal out of Kroft's all-seeing sight. Trying and failing, by inches.

This had all occurred to Lepus in the first ten minutes following his discovery of Poe and Mc-what's-his-face on the TV.

He sat in the dark for some minutes in complete silence, his face as empty as a dime-store mannequin. Without an audience, his mask of emotion was unnecessary. He turned his eyes toward his inner void, a black space that seemed to dwarf everything in its sheer magnitude, and realized without feeling that, somehow, despite its amazing vastness, it was still growing. Soon, he was sure, it would engulf everything. He spent several minutes peering into his depths and saw nothing. Not a shred of humanity. Not a feeling. Not a clear or meaningful memory. Just an empty black plain that stretched on and on and on. Did he really care what happened anymore? Did it really matter? MAJESTIC? NRO DELTA? Poe?

Silence.

Then, for no real reason at all, Lepus picked up the room phone and made some calls of his own.

THE DOOR TO CHARLIE Bostick's room burst open and two shadowy forms blotted out the light of the hallway. So this was it, he thought, just as he always pictured it, a bullet in the head at five o'clock in the morning. No, that wasn't NRO DELTA's style; they would get him somewhere quiet first, away from the hotel. Bostick fumbled on the side table and pushed his glasses on his face.

The two NRO DELTA goons stood at the foot of his bed.

"Get dressed, geek," one said.

"No," Bostick replied.

"What was that?" The other laughed, incredulously.

"I said no. I'm . . . I'm not going to make this easy for you," Bostick said, eyes downcast.

"What the fuck are you talking about?"

"You'll have to kill me here," Bostick whispered. He couldn't believe he was saying the things he was saying. He thought perhaps he was being brave.

Faces blank, the two men simultaneously removed their huge black guns from their jackets and leveled them at Bostick's head. One of the barrels touched Bostick's glasses and chattered there as a wave of tremors moved through his body. He relieved himself there on the bed in one rumbling heave.

Then both men were laughing. The bigger one was laughing so hard he had to sit down and cover his mouth with both hands. The other looked down on Bostick with good-natured contempt. Both had removed their guns from his face and replaced them in their holsters.

"Chill out, Bostick. Lepus wants to see you."

The other man gained control of himself and then looked up, his eyes filled with tears.

"Aw, Jesus, man, that was good."

Shivering uncontrollably, Bostick went into the bathroom, cleaned himself, and got dressed, pulling on whatever clothes he could find there. His mind raced through possibilities. He would never stand up under torture—no one ever did. And if he ended up at OUTLOOK it would be worse, if that were possible; most likely he would never even realize he was being tortured.

He threw his soiled pants in the bathtub and found his eyes fixed on the steel bar that held up the shower curtain. Black thoughts raced between his conscious considerations. Could he hang himself before they could get to him? What would he do to save the world?

One thing seemed clear; the jig was up.

Somehow, he thought, somehow Lepus knew about the God Box. . . .

Part Three: The Architect

"'Imagine that you are creating a fabric of human destiny with the object of making men happy in the end, giving them peace and rest at last, but that it was essential and inevitable to torture to death only one tiny creature—that baby beating its breast with its fist, for instance—and to found that edifice on its unavenged tears, would you consent to be the architect of those conditions? Tell me, and tell the truth.'

"'No I wouldn't consent,' said Alyosha softly."

—Fyodor Dostoyevsky, *The Brothers Karamazov*

"The older order changeth, yielding place to new,
And God fulfills himself in many ways,
Lest one good custom should corrupt the world."

—Alfred Lord Tennyson, *Morte D'Arthur*

Old Friends

Alphonse gets the word: Fairfield Pond, Fairfield, Vermont. 39.93 N/75.18 W latitude/longitude. Approximately 200 miles from Philadelphia, Pennsylvania: Wednesday, February 7, 2001, 7:06 A.M. EST.

JOE CAMP FELT EVERY inch of his eighty-two-year old body groan collectively as he struggled to sit up in bed. It was time to change the damned bag on his hip again. He was a fucking incontinent old man who had fouled things up and he deserved the grief. For the incontinence at least he had an excuse; most of his lower intestine had been removed in surgery after he found himself on the receiving end of a .22 caliber pistol. Things had not healed as they once did. Right now, his body was at war. Every day was a battle.

For the foul-ups he had no excuse except hubris. Hubris, and old-fashioned stupid American pride. The sort they didn't make anymore. It was all apologies and dodges now; no more chin up and out, prepared to bear the consequences of rash actions.

Still, he had things to be grateful for. At least he wasn't a cripple—yet.

He had returned to Fairfield Pond after his extended hospital stay and the debacle that placed Delta Green in hoc with the powers that be. His body, which had once been filled with a quiet murmur of dissent at any strenuous activity, now shrieked in an inhuman chorus of shooting pains and dull aches when he exerted himself in any way, when he so much as walked. But he pushed himself, anyway; there was no other option. The pain was penance. Penance for Reggie, penance for his arrogance. Pain killed his traitorous thoughts before they could turn inward again. Pain dulled the memories that seemed far too old and baroque to ever have been real events at all. What a comfort that was. He could never have done the millions of things that had led to this disgrace; they seemed far too unreal, too strange. No man could have been the architect of such misery and deceit and survived for so long without proper retribution. Retribution for such crimes would have to be death. No other penance was possible. But it wouldn't come.

In his pain, he had built a house here on Fairfield Pond. Not with his own hands, of course. Such projects were long behind him. Locals from Brewster had laid the foundation and done the particulars until it was habitable. Joe had simply done the little things, the finishing touches. Varnishing. Painting. Hanging curtains. These activities ate him up as much as laying a foundation or splitting wood would have done years before. Every night he was a shivering, pain-filled wreck. Too thin and weak to protest when sleep claimed him like the blade of an executioner and kept him for too long. He woke later in the mornings now than he ever had before, and he slept earlier. He no longer had any choice in the matter.

Time no longer felt abundant. It seemed dear, a precious commodity that he could feel slipping away through his hands from moment to moment.

As far as the locals knew, he was one of the far-flung Fairfield clan come back to claim their land after years of abandonment. An heir through marriage who held the proper papers—forged, of course—to keep the local lawyers at bay, and the money necessary to gain the trust and assistance of the nearby townsfolk. No one really even asked his business. Just like Reggie before him, he had found a sort of bitter peace at the lake. A silence found elsewhere only in death.

The lake was like some sort of afterlife.

The new cabin had been built on the opposite side of the lake, away from the ruins of Reggie's cabin, where the patron saint of Delta Green had died. And every morning Joe would rise and look out the window at the collapsed chimney and charred weather-eaten timbers on the other side of the small lake and think:

I'm ready, Reg. We'll trade stories again soon.

You ain't going anywhere, you old fuck, Reggie would answer, a voice from the grave. He still haunted him, even now, seven years dead and buried. What was Reggie to him? An old—what? Friend? Colleague? Maybe. When they had first met in 1953 he would have sworn on a stack of bibles that it would never happen in a million years. They were diametrically opposed in every way. In truth, he was far fonder of Reggie now that he was gone. It was easy to argue with Reggie, now. It was easy to win. In life, as far as he knew, he had never managed to change one single thought in Reggie's stubborn head. No one he could name could complete such a monumental task. Not Reggie's children or ex-wives or the United States government or the things that howl restlessly beyond the veil of reality. Reggie stared them all down equally and ate up his share of pain with a grimace that looked like a smile. He kept it to himself, though, never once looking for respite in his eighty years on the Earth. Joe Camp still had a lot to learn from Reggie. Fighting and dying for what you believed in. Right now such a valiant fate seemed as distant as the moon. Death seemed to be hovering nearby, in a landing pattern, so to speak, waiting for the surrender to age and infirmity that it could sense was coming.

Soon enough. Soon enough.

God knew he deserved to die. For Adam. For Shasta—Agent Shasta, David Foster Nells, whose mother had fired the shots that nearly killed Camp. For every single one he had sent into the fire without a second thought and had written off like a trifle. Too concerned with the big picture, too ready to risk valuable personnel on intelligence-gathering operations. Perhaps Reggie had been right, after all. Find it, kill it, and cover it up. The old way, the cowboy way. When it worked, it worked well; but otherwise it was inevitably a disaster. We can't kill what we can't find, he had argued so long ago. And Reggie had said:

When the real shit flies, it isn't hard to find it.

This was true enough.

Joe Camp discarded the colostomy bag and replaced it with a fresh one, taking a moment to consider the long, bright pink scars that surrounded the stoma hole in his puckered, ruined abdomen like crevasses. In a way, he was amazed he had survived at all. The time after the shooting was a hazy, pain-filled dream rich with the metallic taste of opiates and blood in his mouth. For a time he had thought perhaps the hospital was the afterlife, but that dim hope had faded with the drugs.

He rose back into the world, as it really was; a world without heroes.

Delta Green was gone. The organization he had painstakingly constructed, from the cowboy network of its previous incarnation to an organized conspiracy, was now in the pocket of its worst enemy. MAJESTIC pulled the strings and the conspiracy danced like a marionette, cutting jigs for reasons it could never know. To those inside, it went on in its former incarnation. But to those in the know, it seemed a terrible parody of what it once had been. It seemed set in stone, now, that it would forever be a tool of MAJESTIC, nothing more than another of the many tendrils of power the MAJESTIC Steering Committee wielded within the United States. No maneuver or feint he could concoct seemed to have any hope of restoring the conspiracy to its former effectiveness. It was gone and that was that.

Worse yet, Joe had let it go. He hadn't the willpower or strength to fight the change as Gavin Ross slipped into place as the new leader of the conspiracy, completing a daring and clever maneuver as Delta Green was at its weakest point in more than thirty years. What could Joe do?

The best he could do was watch and hang on to those few agents he knew to be loyal to their cause. Experienced agents who knew what was what. Everyone else was an unwitting pawn of MAJESTIC. So far, his attempts to control the rather public incidents of the last few weeks had proven too little, too late. His seven operating agents, a skeleton crew to be sure, could not handle the caseload, and two of them were already gone, possibly dead, missing amidst the biggest murder investigation in Pennsylvania police history. There were not enough hands to go around, to cover up their moves, to smooth over all the bumps. The agents were alone in the field and exposed. None of the friendlies known to the conspiracy before the takeover could be trusted completely.

His mind still fiddled with the problem unconsciously, a nagging, recurring thought which would not go no matter how hard he tried to banish it from his mind. How could he restore the conspiracy? There was always a way. Surrender was never the final option. Success was a measure of degree. Any degree of victory is a victory, no matter how minor. This voice nagged him and rode him. He thought maybe it was Reggie's voice.

Joe pushed himself out of bed and began his hour-long ritual of preparing for the day. Most of his time seemed to be eaten up by mundane activities. Shaving. Dressing. Pointless, repetitive actions that served only tiny, inconsequential ends now ruled his life. They made the rest of his world, the time he spent actually doing things, seem far too limited to be of any use.

He made it halfway through his ritual, and had managed to pull on his pants, when a loud buzzer sounded, startling him—the sound of the intercom being rung at the east gate. The gate from the highway. Camp puttered over to the door and intercom with a sloth-like slowness, trying to appease the pains that rushed through his body like sudden, randomly placed blades of ice. Anyone watching him would have cringed, reacting to the expressions of pain that rippled across his face as he shifted his feet slowly along the wood floor.

"Yes," he said into the intercom, wheezing a little, depressing the button with a huge calloused thumb.

"Open up, Joe," Forrest James asked in a somber, withdrawn voice.

Joe Camp stood still for a time, looking at the little white box of the intercom, trying to stare into it and see Forrest on the other end. Clean-shaven, chiseled Forrest. Traitor Forrest. The Benedict Arnold of the conspiracy. He was like a son to Joe. A prodigal son. But a lot had changed in the months since Forrest James had gone on the run, a fugitive escaped from Leavenworth.

Gavin Ross had taken James in, given him a place within MAJESTIC, given him a mission. Maybe James thought he was doing it for the sake of Delta Green. But that didn't matter. Gavin Ross had twisted James like an amateur, filling his head with lies and propaganda, shifting his allegiances to MAJESTIC's ends. Now there was no difference between James and the enemy. Camp's most valued pupil had strayed from the track and been consumed. There was only the enemy now. James was gone.

Gone.

It seemed death was much more prompt and courteous than Camp had ever given it credit for. In all his years, he had never heard it announce itself before. After all, most likely James was here to end it all. To wrap up the old conspiracy in a nice, big, blood-red bow and hand it over to Ross like a birthday gift.

But Camp had learned a few things from Reggie. A few things which would hasten the end of MAJESTIC along—if such a group could ever be destroyed—even if it only meant taking a few with him when he went. Reggie had taken eight men with him the night they came for him. Eight of the best. Camp planned to one-up him. He wanted to brag about it if he ever saw him again. God knew it took a lot to shut Reggie up.

Joe smiled faintly, eyes unfocused and far away. It was amazing how the concept of the afterlife seemed to gain ground and credence in your mind as death approached. It was true; there were no atheists in foxholes.

CLICK. "Joe?" The intercom asked again, quietly.

Joe Camp checked the big black pistol at his hip. His blunt, arthritic hands fumbled with the action and cocked it. He had carried the gun through Burma and the Philippines, through the Gibson Desert of Australia and the steppes of China. Over the past fifty-eight years it had fired at men and it had fired at monsters. In a way, it was his oldest and most loyal friend.

He always wore his pistol; that was part of his ritual, too.

Like the Mafia, they had sent family to see him off, a friend with a smile to distract from the knife. A friend to make him weak and then exploit the weakness. But maybe this was his chance to make things right. To even the equation. Two traitors gone in one go. Himself, a traitor to his compatriots within the conspiracy, and James—well, James was worse. It looked like it'd come out a bit more than even.

Yes, he had things to be thankful for, as few and far between as they were.

Joe Camp depressed the gate-release button and hurried, as best he could, to find his end.

FORREST JAMES STOOD NEXT to an anonymous black 4x4 dressed in black himself, like a bad guy from a funny book. He had entered and closed the gate behind him, parking the immense vehicle diagonally across the dirt road. No one else, apparently, was present. A cloud of dust slowly settled in the thin January air.

James' huge hands were held stiffly at his sides and he considered Camp with an expression of concern. The old man did his best to hobble up the uneven dirt road, and his best was not very good at all. Camp stumbled once and James started forward unconsciously, but something in James' flat blue eyes hardened and he held himself back. Camp didn't fall, and continued on his way, dragging his feet in an exhausted pace. When James saw the old .45 in Camp's hand, he raised his hands in a sign of surrender.

James' eyes were wide, not with fear but with something like detached concern.

"I'm not here to collect, Joe. I've got some news," James announced loudly.

The two men stood more than fifty feet apart. Joe's yellowed eyes tracked the tree line slowly on either side of the road, searching for targets. When he was reasonably sure they were alone, he turned back to consider the man that Forrest James had become.

James looked harder than he had ever been before, as if he was sculpted from stone in stark geometric lines like some Soviet monument. Just past fifty, he looked in better shape than most men half his age. His blond hair was cropped painfully short, revealing a gleaming pink scalp beneath. Joe thought maybe he had cut it to hide the grey that was visible at his temples. Or was that just a foolish thought? An attempt to belittle the man Joe had once thought of as a son? He thought maybe it was.

There was a wedding ring on his finger. A simple gold band.

"Stephanie?" Joe murmured, gesturing with the pistol towards James' left hand.

"Yeah." Forrest smiled and fiddled with the ring for a moment. For a moment it was the James he knew. He could feel the hidden warmth, the good heart buried in a chest that was naked without body armor. The uneven, closed-mouth grin.

Then the feeling was gone.

"Ross wants me to fill you in on some . . . developments," James stated simply.

"You his lapdog now?" Joe spat back.

"Let's not get into this, Joe. Not now."

Joe sighed.

"Go ahead. Get it over with. What do you have to say?"

"Ross wants Lepus out of the way. Consider him a gift. Retribution for Shasta."

"And we're supposed to be your hit men now?"

"It's not like that. Ross is sure that Lepus is on some sort of crusade. He's after someone named Poe. He was overheard shouting about it before he left. Ross thinks Poe may be involved with Delta Green. Does that mean anything to you?"

"Maybe."

"C'mon, Joe, this is a favor. You know you want him."

"Donald Poe is agent Charlie."

James' expression shifted. His thick eyebrows rose in surprise.

"I—" James began, but Joe cut him off.

"You know him, yes. You two worked on an operation in 1991, in California." Joe was lost in thought. The gun hung forgotten in his hand.

"He's a good man."

"Yes. One of the few," Camp said.

James began to say something but fell silent. Wind rustled the dead trees in a noise like a whisper.

"Anyway." James tossed a thick, padded manila envelope wrapped in plastic in the dirt in the middle of the road. "That's all you need to find Lepus, twenty-four/seven. I trust you'll take care of it."

"I'll do what I need to do."

James began to turn away, but stopped with his back to Joe.

"Lepus knows Poe?"

"They were both on OBSIDIAN in 1969. They were both there when it all fell apart."

"Jesus. You never would have known. Charlie was solid," James said, mostly to himself, looking at the sky.

"Is solid," Joe sharply corrected.

"Yes. But for how long, with Lepus on his tail?"

"Get out of here, Forrest. You give my love to Stephanie. At least she has an excuse. She fell in love with the wrong man. You, on the other hand. . . ."

"What?"

"She fell in love with a man, that's excusable. You fell in love with power. It'll eat you up and spit you out, and it'll take her with you. Don't forget I said that."

"Anything else, Joe?" Forrest sighed as he laid his huge hands on the gate.

"Yeah. Get off my property before I shoot you, you asshole."

The man Forrest James had become opened the gate, got in his 4x4 and left without looking back.

Hello, Goodbye

Lepus finds the trail: Rent-N-Save, Interstate 95, Philadelphia, Pennsylvania. 39.93 N/75.18 W latitude/longitude. Approximately 200 miles from Fairfield, Vermont: Wednesday, February 7, 2001, 8:39 P.M. EST.

NRO DELTA DESCENDED ON the area around the Rent-N-Save on Interstate 95 like locusts swarming a field of fresh wheat. A dozen black vans swept up the pot-holed cement of all three entrances to the facility simultaneously. A silent helicopter swept low over the compound, twice covering the facility in a clear white light, circling low, scanning for targets. A near-freezing rain spilled from the sky in spits and starts.

Lepus had learned a few tricks, ways to flush the quail out of the brush. The quail in this particular situation was Delta Green.

Lepus knew a lot about Delta Green. He had been a member himself, once, before he went to greener pastures, so to speak. He had encountered them a time or three since then in NRO DELTA's clean-up operations. He understood their propensity for storage facilities. He had seen that trick cleaning up after Groversville. That was the kind of place Poe would go to ground.

That narrowed things down a little.

Poe had replaced his rented car with a stolen one. Three had been liberated in the area around the abandoned rental car on the night of the shootout. One was a rotting red Mustang, which was found after a prolonged helicopter search of all the storage facilities in the Philadelphia metropolitan area.

Poe was good. Efficient.

Lepus was better.

The front and back gates were blown simultaneously and a rush of black-suited commandos swept into the lot, skirting buildings, MP5 submachine guns trained in every possible direction, covering all the angles. Two men rushed to the red Mustang parked in front of unit 31 and removed the keys from its ignition.

"Blood here, Command," the commando murmured into his mike.

"We got 'em," Lepus cackled from inside the command van outside the facility, and clapped his hands together. "I want 'em alive, you hear me, Nine? It's them alive or you dead, you copy that?" The com operator in the van looked at Lepus with something like religious ecstasy and smiled.

"Yes, sir," Nine replied, unfazed.

Eleven men closed in around unit 31, an anonymous green shed. It was closed, identical to the ninety-seven other buildings in the lot.

"Set it up," Nine commanded.

Two men unfolded a small green device with a small dish that looked a little like a satellite uplink. They aimed the dish at the plain steel garage door of the unit.

"DULCE ready, sir. On your command."

"Go," Lepus barked.

The only thing that indicated the device had been activated was a low humming, which shook nearby objects in rising waves of rapid vibration. The commandos stood nearby, all behind the device, teeth clenched as it cycled up and then slowly back down again.

"Kill it."

The device clicked off and a second later everything nearby stopped shaking. The last thing to stop shaking was the garage door, which came to a stuttering stop with a loud clang.

"No reaction inside. No heat targets," Nine reported.

"Open it," Lepus murmured into the mike.

The door was swept open by two men while four poured in with their night vision gear on. The cluttered room held no living targets.

"No targets. No targets," Nine reported.

"What the fuck is in there?" Lepus said.

"Cartons. Some weapons. Papers," Nine replied.

On the video feed, a NRO man held one of the pieces of paper. It was a photocopied sheet with simple lettering. It read "HELLO, GOODBYE," and hundreds of them were scattered around the room. Lepus froze in the van, the submachine gun in one hand, his body armor half on. The smile faded from his face slowly. His eyes opened wide.

Lepus snatched the mike off the com operator's head. "GET OUT OF THERE!" he shrieked into it.

"Sir—"

The explosion was sudden, but not unexpected.

The van was swept to the side like the hand of an invisible giant had given it a disinterested swat. It hit a cement abutment and toppled, rolling twice out onto Interstate 95, which was luckily empty of traffic. Lepus felt weightless for a moment. The com operator rose from his seat in slow motion like a magic trick, floating towards the ceiling in a sitting position. Papers in the van floated up into the air; the microphone headset swam upwards like a fragile sea creature heading toward the light of the surface. Then the main shockwave and sound hit the van and everything went to pieces.

The lights in the van cut out when it completed its first tumble. Its left side crumpled like an aluminum can, with a shriek of twisting metal. The roar was beyond conception. Everything in the van vibrated terribly. Lepus bit his tongue and felt blood well up in his mouth like a wave of molten copper. Bulletproof windows blew inwards, spraying the cabin with squared fragments of resin, stinging his face and hands. A wave of heat penetrated the van like X rays.

As the van rolled a second time, Lepus struck the floor roughly and then the ceiling a second later, like a rock being tumbled to smoothness in an enormous machine. He released the submachine gun in midair and vaguely heard it impact the floor and the ceiling, just before he did the same things. Bones in his left hand popped audibly as he landed on the ceiling, but he felt no pain. His shoulders bore the brunt of the force as he tumbled end over end. Unconsciously he rolled and curled up into a ball. He had trained in jump school, after all; he was no idiot.

A shuddering; skidding slide across pavement, the entire van upside down. Sparks floated past the window like a snowfall of fire.

Silence.

Then, as if heard through a pillow, muffled radio traffic.

Lepus pulled himself to his feet and retrieved an MP5 from next to the dead com operator, forcing his bruised fingers into the trigger guard with a grimace. The radioman's neck was bent like a snapped matchstick and his eyes were wide with shock.

Lepus kicked the door open with a boot and stumbled out into the road.

A wall of blazing buildings lit the night to the west, the remnants of what had once been Rent-N-Save. Now it looked like Hell. A plume of black and grey smoke split the night sky like the hand of God himself, surrounded by a sheet of fire forty feet high.

Then the debris started to come down.

The first shingle of steel missed Lepus by less than five feet, scything its way into the pavement. He beat a rapid retreat into the overturned van as the rest came down, and he recovered a super fiberglass helmet from the storage locker. He sat in the van, hunched down, watching the ruins fall from the sky.

Sixty, eighty pounds of C4. Something like that.

A tire, burning wood planks, steel plating and, twice, body parts came down, most smoldering or completely incinerated by the destruction, hitting the cement with dull thuds, one after another.

Finally, Lepus emerged into the night.

Someone had given him up. Someone had squealed. He could guess it was Ross—but what did it matter, really? He was at war. With MAJESTIC in all its forms, but most of all, with Poe. Poe was good when Lepus had known him. Apparently he had just kept getting better and better, like a fucking fine wine. Maybe he was the best. Who knew? The score was certainly skewed in Poe's favor now. Twelve to zero. Nothing in the compound was going to come walking out. Maybe he even got the ZEUS copter. Who knew?

And who cared?

"YOU MISSED ME, YOU OLD FUCK!" Lepus shrieked into the night sky, submachine gun in his ruined hand. His laughter was rich and full and true.

It was the first real thing besides fear that Adolph Lepus had felt in a long time.

Deals

Alphonse makes a social call: Hotel Dreyfus, Philadelphia, Pennsylvania. 39.93 N/75.18 W latitude/longitude. Approximately 9 miles from Interstate 95: Friday, February 9, 2001, 10:15 A.M. EST.

A KNOCK AT THE door. Lepus leapt up off the bed, covered in sweat, and almost discharged the pistol in his hand. It would have put a nice big hole through the door and whatever was on the other side. Why he stopped was just as much a mystery as why he wanted to do it in the first place. Such considerations no longer seemed significant to him, or even possible.

He wiped his face in the dark with his bandaged, shattered hand. There were dreams behind his eyes that would not go away. Whistling nightmares calling to him with convoluted alien tunes. Slowly, however, the tunes were becoming clearer, melodies as familiar as the songs his mother sang to him as a child. The more he slept, the more he saw. He thought maybe it was all coming clear, finally. OBSIDIAN and the incident at OUTLOOK. The way the real world could slip away like water tumbling down a hole, draining away to reveal the gleaming and polished surface of eternity.

The night at Fairfield Pond. . . .

"What?" he barked.

"Sir," one of his men said through the door, "there's an old man downstairs asking for you at the registry desk." Absurdly, his first thought was that it was Reginald Fairfield, returned from the grave to get his due.

"Ross?" Lepus murmured. Was it possible the man was that stupid?

"No, sir. Older than that. He says he knows you—he used your real name."

"What does this geezer look like?" Lepus pulled the door open distractedly and turned his back immediately on his man, who stood stock still, as if he was expecting a blow to fall any minute from some random and unseen assailant. Lepus retrieved a fresh black jacket from the closet and slipped it on over his body armor and shoulder rig.

"He looks like a pissed-off Shriner," the man confessed, sounding unsure.

"Joe," Lepus said, mostly to himself, and smiled.

The NRO DELTA man at the door had done things. He had shot children and old women and burned houses filled with innocents to the ground. He had removed teeth with pliers and bent fingers back until they weren't fingers anymore, just sausage-lumps of split flesh. He had dodged bullets in banana republics and missed fiery death by inches, dozens, no, hundreds of times. But when Lepus smiled at him, he shivered.

"What's the matter, son?" Lepus grinned. "Goose walk over your grave?"

Lepus waltzed out without saying another word and the NRO DELTA man followed as best he could. It was impossible to follow Lepus very far down his particular path; only a select few could even see it. That path veered off the straight and narrow so long ago the trail had long since grown over with brambles and stickers. There was nothing down his path but death in all its forms, death and death and more death. As long as he was the architect of such misery, Lepus often thought, that was enough to keep him moving forward.

JOE CAMP SQUATTED UNCOMFORTABLY on a beige, high-backed chair in the lobby, looking like an elderly raven. His face was a mess of lines of age and pain. His blue eyes had lost their sheen and were glazed with a thin sheet of nicotine yellow. There was a paper on his lap. The old man had his hand under it.

It was a big paper.

Lepus glided over to him after waving off his men. In the lobby, life continued apace. No one could tell that world-affecting events were about to unfold. Lepus' eyes were fixed on the newspaper on Joe Camp's lap.

"And me without my gun. How embarrassing," Lepus giggled. He patted his jacket and made a comical face, "Oh, wait. There it is. The missus must have packed it." He dropped lithely into the chair next to Joe with a thump, smiling all the while.

"Enough of this shit, Adolph," Joe said.

"Why, Joe, so short with your old friend?"

"We were never friends, Adolph."

"I know, but it doesn't mean I'm not trying."

"Shut up."

"Fine, we'll do it your way. Reggie'd be proud: 'What's the time in Tokyo?'" Lepus giggled again, hunching down to match Camp's stature, his face shifted into a contortion of flesh, his lips pursed and eyebrows drawn down to a squint.

Joe's free hand seized Lepus' bandaged hand like a coiled snake. The meaty, blunt fingers squeezed hard. Bones within ground together slowly. Lepus squirmed, but his face did not change, except for one thing. His eyebrows rose slightly in a look of surprise.

"Now shut up and listen, you fairy," Joe hissed. He released Lepus' hand suddenly, which jerked away from the old man seemingly of its own accord.

"You still got it, old man." Lepus shook his head and whistled, grinning.

"Listen: Ross gave you up to me."

"Oh, really?" Lepus' eyes drifted away. He leaned back in the chair and crossed his long legs, obviously bored.

"Listen!" Joe shouted.

People turned to look at the odd sight. Children stopped playing near the elevator, mothers shook their heads and glanced at the old man and the man in black. The two NRO DELTA suits stood, alert, ready to spring at any moment.

Then the moment ended and people looked away again.

"Drawing attention is not a good plan, Joe," Lepus chided.

"I don't want you anymore, Adolph. That's the kicker. I don't want you. I want to give you something, something you want. And in exchange—" Joe was wheezing, and sweat coated his face. The unpleasant metallic smell of it rose off him in waves.

Lepus turned back to consider Camp with something like confusion.

"Joe, what happened to you in that hospital? Dealing with the enemy?"

"There are bigger considerations."

"You've said as much already. Get on with it. I have things to do."

"I can give you Poe."

The moment stretched out like taffy. Then, slowly, Lepus' face split down the middle with his gold-toothed smile.

"And what would make you do that, Joe? What would I have to do?"

"Something you want to do already."

"I'm still here."

"Kroft. I want Kroft," Joe whispered, watching the two NRO DELTA goons across the room with wary eyes.

Lepus glanced around as if they could have been overheard.

"Are you crazy? He's not even human anymore."

"You'll never get Poe without me."

"Shit. You don't need to tell me that. He almost got me last night."

"That explosion near the airport?" Joe asked.

"Yeah, that was him."

"I thought so. That's why I want him gone," Camp finished.

"I see...."

"How do I know you won't turn on the deal? You kill Kroft first, then I give you Poe."

"How do I know *you* won't turn on the deal?" Lepus replied.

"How many more explosions and shoot-outs can we survive? How long before we're all in front of the firing squad?"

"I see."

Lepus stood up suddenly and left Joe sitting.

"Where can I get through to you?"

Joe Camp snickered and then Lepus joined him. Both knew a second meeting would go very differently. "No, Adolph. Not now."

They stared at each for a long time.

"Deal," Lepus finally said, smiling, as always.

They shook on it, and Joe squeezed Lepus' bruised fingers with obvious relish.

Joe began to waddle out when Lepus dropped a long, thin hand on his shoulder.

"Y'know, Joe, in case I don't get to see you again, I have to tell you I've always enjoyed your particular brand of melodrama. I hope I'm the main antagonist when this whole thing gets through. I hate playing second fiddle to Kroft."

"Don't worry. I'll keep my top slot clean. There's always time for one more dance," Camp spat back and walked away, shaking Lepus' hand off his shoulder.

Lepus looked after the old man as he exited, eyes full of quiet wonder and admiration.

The Sound of Infinity

Kroft does some detective work: The "Country Club," outside Mount Weather, Virginia. 38.98 N/76.50 W latitude/longitude. Approximately 96 miles from Philadelphia, Pennsylvania: Friday, February 9, 2001, 1:12 P.M. EST.

JUSTIN KROFT SAT IN his huge office and considered the playback on the immense flat screen embedded in the cream-colored wall opposite him. The screen was split between two video images, time-coded. On the left side of the screen, Adolph Lepus rushed into a hospital room where a man lay in the bed with a blank look on his face, while a sound played in the background; a distant, rising and falling tone, a strange melody of what sounded like flutes, a million of them, weaving together to occasionally form a perfect, haunting tune.

On the second screen, a shaking, static-blurred recording from Colonel Coffey's helmet cam showed a vast fleshy thing struggling to pull him down into the depths of a basement. There, too, a bizarre melody played, rising and falling just at the edge of the recording. MAJESTIC analysts had timed the recordings so that the sounds in the background were brought into synchronization.

The two tunes, separated by more than a year, by thousands of miles, and by circumstance, were the same.

The Nells incident at OUTLOOK Group B and the thing in the basement in Seattle were connected. But how?

"Prompt," Kroft murmured. A screen embedded in the desk lit up, displaying a computer desktop.

"Open file Nells, David F." The screen jumped instantly to a case file.

"Correlate with personnel file Coffey, Colonel Robert."

"Coffey, Colonel Robert J., deceased?" The computer asked in a female voice as smooth as honey.

"Yes," Kroft said, and took his glasses off.

A second later there was a beep.

"Seven verbatim word or phrase matches, no factual matches, no known heredity link, no known social link," the computer chirped.

"List, please."

"Three matches: 'Robert.' One match: 'Black Taurus.' Two matches: 'Annapolis, Maryland.' One match: 'Mother.' No other matches."

Kroft sighed. Nothing linked the two in any way that MAJESTIC could uncover; this little game with the computer was just a last bit of ego waxing through his thin veneer of calm. What the hell was the connection?

There was some link.

Today, at 69 years of age, Justin Kroft looked better than he ever had in the last twenty years. His cancer had gone into complete remission, nearly instantly, though few in his organization had known of it in the first place. It had not been some miracle of his immune system that had brought him back to this youthful state from the precipice of cancerous death. Kroft had plundered alien science for his current vigor. But even that could fade at any moment. His "modifications" seemed to be working well enough, but the tricks and traps hidden in the "Cookbook," the collection of secrets handed over by the aliens, were not reliable. At any moment he could find his colon cancer growing malignantly again—or worse, he could end up like the residents of Groversville, controlled from within by the Greys, or whatever was behind the Greys.

It was quite possible that what had been done to him by MAJESTIC scientists at Facility-12 could never be undone. And it required so many treatments. What had once been a twice-a-year jaunt to Montana had grown to twice a month, and now four times monthly. Those silent few who administered his treatments at Facility-12 were completely in his pocket, and outside them, none in the tight-knit organization knew anything about it. He was told that as long as the treatments continued, his lifespan was indefinite, theoretically infinite. But how long before some jealous lackey brought his treatments to the attention of the Steering Committee? How long until his enemies made a move against him, utilizing this weakness?

Nells was immune to all that. He had stepped past the bounds of humanity and had become something else. He was invulnerable, immortal and perfect.

Nells was like a god. He was free of all earthly encumbrances. The immortality Kroft had found was nothing but a hollow shadow of what Nells had, what he had seemingly gained without effort or foreknowledge.

Kroft very badly wanted to be that way. That's why he had pushed the research forward, despite all the dangers that became apparent when the first reports of Nells' amazing abilities began to come out of OUTLOOK.

OUTLOOK had seen such things before, of course, but never on the level of Nells, never even a percentage of what Nells could do so effortlessly. The others had been dissected and studied and tested and prodded. Nells had simply sat back quietly until something touched a nerve, and then he lashed out, leveling all in his path with only the power of his mind.

What Yrjo and his teams had recovered was only enough to confirm that Nells was exactly what Kroft wanted to be—that, and nothing else. The measurements of Nells' abilities—off the scale of human knowledge—mocked Kroft. The limitless and perfect power seemed forever beyond his reach.

It was somehow a natural thing. In some way that no one, not even MAJESTIC, could understand, Nells simply could will these things into reality.

"Off," Kroft murmured. The screen vanished, leaving the desktop vacant and black.

"Screen." The screen on the far wall fell blank and silent.

"Dim lights," and the lights dimmed.

He sat in darkness for a very long time.

The silence was broken by a beep.

"Sir, the jet is ready," a quiet, gravelly voice intoned over the hidden speaker.

Although he was loath to do so, and felt like he had already lived a thousand years, Justin Kroft raised himself up and got ready to go to Montana. His will to live had become nothing more than a need to frustrate his opponents in the game he called life.

The Bare Bones of It

McRay gets the word: The Wilson Motel, 220 Carter Street, Philadelphia, Pennsylvania. 39.93 N/75.18 W latitude/longitude. Approximately 96 miles from Mount Weather, Virginia: Saturday, February 10, 2001, 1:06 P.M. EST.

"CURTIS."

The voice seeped in from above, as if from a great distance. Drifting through a gauzy, grey, indistinct haze. The sound of his name found something in his mind and he stirred. With this change, the pain rose up in a great red wave, trying to push him back down, trying to drown him. Something in him wanted to let go, to give up and sink back into the depths, but his mind swam toward the surface of consciousness, and his eyes fluttered open. It felt like surfacing from the silent, silt-covered bottom of a deep, cool lake into a world on fire.

Blurry, Poe crouched before him, uncomfortably squatting on his haunches, eyes peering intently into his own. The old man looked haggard.

"How bad?" McRay asked. His voice sounded washed-out and weak.

"It's under control. You're going to make it," Poe said, looking back over his shoulder. McRay could not see clearly past a few feet. A blinding yellow light glowed from over the enormous man's shoulders. Someone moved past it, blocking the unearthly light for a few seconds, like a cloud passing over the sun.

"Who?" was all that McRay could manage.

"A Friendly. No worries. Take it easy. Curtis, listen to me. I got to go—" Poe looked torn. His face was a mask of emotion.

"What?" McRay said, the world fading in and out in cycles of deep, red pain.

"Lepus is on to us. He'll find us before too long, unless. . . ." Poe stood and snatched up his duffel bag.

McRay's thin hand rose slowly, although he could not feel it, and snagged Poe's pants leg. It dropped away, unable to hold on.

"Don't," McRay choked.

"I have to, Curtis. It's long overdue." Poe gently lifted McRay's limp arm and folded it across his chest.

"You'll kill each other. . . ." The sentence was a struggle in itself. McRay's voice died in the middle of it.

"That's the bare bones of it." Poe turned to walk away.

"Wait," McRay whispered.

Poe turned back, noting the change in his tone. McRay waved a hand covered with dried blood at Poe, to come closer.

Poe leaned down until he was less than foot away. The old man's face came into sharp focus, a strong square face covered in a spider's nest of wrinkles. His blue eyes searched McRay's with concern. There was something final in that look, like the closing lines of a novel.

"You're off to kill the devil," McRay hissed. "Don't give him a chance to shoot back. Cap the fucker. Shoot him in the back. Don't confront him. Assassinate him." McRay felt the world swim away on a tide of pain. When his eyes refocused, Poe had already turned to walk away, nothing more than a hulking shadow backlit by the unearthly light through the windows.

"Don't let him out of your sight. He's the last person I trust," he heard Poe tell the other person in the room, but it had become difficult to concentrate. Time seemed to slip its tether, and the world spiraled away like a cord unwinding from a spool falling in the black. The world was the red of pain and the black of the void. His vision sputtered between the two extremes, shuttering away quicker and quicker until only the pain remained.

After an eternity a woman's voice responded, "I won't."

"Luck," McRay croaked, a barely audible prayer, then fell into the black.

POE HAD GOTTEN THE word from Alphonse just hours before that Lepus was on the move, and was now, apparently, open game. It had bounced through countless electronic channels before finding its way to his cell phone, the news of Lepus' defection.

Better news he had not heard in a long time—if it was true. Right now, the only person he fully trusted was laid out with a bullet hole in his leg. The conspiracy was split between the old guard— still led by Alphonse—and the new guard masquerading as the old guard. Who the new guard was, Poe didn't know, and Alphonse wouldn't say. But he had his suspicions.

MAJESTIC had given Lepus up. A general alert had been sent through the rerouter, along with a rather curious web address. Lepus had become Delta Green's enemy number one. Dozens of agents and friendlies would be gunning for him now. A few had even dealt with him before.

Poe had checked out the information less than two hours before at a rinky-dink coffee house on an old and beaten Dell computer for a dollar fifty an hour. A web address, an eleven-digit code, and voilà: What purported to be an up-to-the minute map-track of Lepus' location, twenty-four/seven, popped up on the screen.

Poe had no doubt that MAJESTIC was capable of such a feat— he had witnessed the horror of Groversville with his own eyes—but he did not blindly trust what he saw there, either. It was an interesting possibility, nothing more. But he would proceed—with caution—as if it was absolute truth. Just. In. Case.

Poe hopped in the rental van and considered the prize he had sprung from the Green Box in Dennison, Pennsylvania, the night before: a huge Barrett .50 caliber sniper rifle with an enormous starscope.

At 1,000 yards, the rifle could punch a hole the size of a human head through cinder block.

Poe imagined Lepus' gaunt, pale face cemented in the glowing crosshairs of the scope, and an unconscious smile drifted onto his lips. He imagined the spray of bone, blood, and gristle as the psychopath's head popped like a zit, leaving a stumbling corpse behind.

"Bang," Poe whispered, almost like a prayer of his own, and drove away.

Safeguards

Lepus makes his move: Facility-12, outside Billings, Montana. 38.98 N/76.50 W latitude/longitude. Approximately 1,106 miles from Philadelphia, Pennsylvania: Friday, February 9, 2001, 6:43 P.M. CST.

IT HAD FINALLY HAPPENED: doom delivered in a Southern drawl, floating down the secure cell line like a black stain on the horizon.

He was a switchman, hovering at the edge of the organization, waiting for the word. And now that it had come, he felt neither elation nor fear, but something like surprise, like the kid in the missile silo hearing that red phone ring for the last time. It was something he thought might never come, but now that it was here he knew there was no going back. The world that had existed minutes before was gone. There was only the future, now a countdown, and his orders.

Supervisory Special Agent Grant of NRO Section Delta knew there were reasons for everything. Reasons within reasons. In his time with the group, he had learned only a few of the secrets no one knows. But the first secret he learned was the greatest: that knowing more was not always a good thing.

The group was what stood between the illusion of the world and the reality that hovered beneath it. This reality was elusive. Everything was there to make you miss it. The entire world was drawn taut across something that writhed and moved and swam. Sometimes it congealed and took you under; sometimes it had teeth. The powers that be had put him to the task. It was his job to find it, root it out and maintain the illusion that nothing besides the everyday world was real.

It had not always been his job. He once had worked for the government.

In 1986, he was suddenly transferred from the SEALs to a cushy job at the obscure and secretive National Reconnaissance Office.

Rumors persisted that the NRO was not what it seemed—that it did more than run the country's satellites—and that it was so near the top of the military totem pole that to see the Office of the President you had to look down.

His friends mocked him; even he had to admit it was ridiculous. Reading maps, planning, sitting at a desk for a living, it was totally and completely foreign to him. The idea of Grant, a man once described as "monolithic," sitting at a desk was as surprising and ridiculous as an ape playing blackjack or a nun wearing six-shooters. Grant didn't know what to make of the transfer, except there was an astronomical pay raise. He did as he was told. It was a promotion, of sorts, and in the government those who did not take promotions were not long for their jobs. Of course, this was before he learned that even the government was an illusion, a shell hiding something secret inside. Something in him told him to take it, to see what it was like to call the shots for a change. Instead of being shot at, he could direct who was shot.

It turned out far different from the scenarios he had imagined in the weeks before the move. There was a desk—which he saw perhaps a half a dozen times—in an anonymous facility on deniable land forty miles from Washington, D.C. But besides that, nothing really fit the images he had conjured in his weeks of waiting. Security at the facility was so complete that Grant felt even the words he spoke were rationed and allotted to him. Eye scans, hand scans, voice maps, number codes. Challenges and responses. By comparison, it made the ironclad security at Fort Detrick's top secret Army Medical Weapons Research facility look like a door kicked off its hinges and then gingerly balanced back on the ruined frame.

For a few weeks he was tested, questioned, poked and prodded. It was less physically stressful than his SEAL training had been, but it required a quick mind. He was given protocols that read like legal jargon, orders that were vague, commands that were questionable, and personality tests that looked like those things women filled out in the back of *Cosmopolitan* magazine. He did it all: spat back his orders while taking a dump; repeated baffling protocols at two in the morning to a voice behind a blinding flashlight; and when suddenly given the order to beat three armed guards into submission with a five-pound flashlight, he had complied with cautious aplomb. His superiors—who all looked exactly alike; that is, just like him—seemed nonplussed. An experienced SEAL, he knew this was the highest compliment such men were capable of giving. They would never let you off the hook; they could only choose not to smile while you dangled. To such men, this was the equivalent of a standing ovation.

He was placed with a field team fourteen months after his transfer. Still unsure just what the group did, Grant followed directions and did his best to not make waves. When he actually realized what they were to do—though not why, not yet—he was surprised to find it was not what he had imagined.

The job included far more gunplay than he would have thought possible for a desk job.

For the next ten years he worked as a bodyguard, courier, and security man for NRO DELTA, a group so secret and insular that no one of his rank knew precisely to whom they reported. Reports went up the very short chain—from Special Agent to Supervisory Special Agent to Section Chief Lepus—and vanished. Directives rained down in return like hailstones. It was like those old jungle movies: The natives worshipped a deity they could never see; the priests made offerings to it, poorly understood gifts to the invisible and all-powerful being by whose grace alone they existed; and occasionally the mountain spat back fire. It was dangerous and exciting, and it beat the hell out of the hurry-up-and-wait lifestyle of the SEALs.

He learned things about the group in the same way plants

absorb carbon dioxide. He stood near conversations, accidentally memorized papers that he saw for a split second, and occasionally murdered someone who in the last fifteen seconds of life babbled about flying saucers and aliens and the end of the world. It was surprising how much a person could get across in those last fifteen seconds—he never gave them more time, no matter what they said, though some said some pretty startling things. He knew if he listened too long, he would be sucked in. The stories were mostly of the same mold, things you associated with late-night creature features or bad TV. Still, it was hard to discount them. The first, maybe; but after nine or ten guys like that under your belt, all parroting a similar tune, it was hard not to start humming it yourself.

After all, nothing gives credence to a madman's insane babbling like the fact that you have been dispatched to kill him late at night, along with twelve other killers that cost roughly four million dollars to train apiece, in a sound-dampened Black Hawk M-29a helicopter packed with technology so advanced that it would make Mr. Wizard lose his lunch.

As far as he knew, the group that called the shots was a government unto itself. A government within the government. It was obvious the area between the "real" government and that of the group was no longer in dispute. Those who wandered into that wasteland in between—the area that held back the secrets of the group inside like the membrane of a cell—became the missing and the abandoned dead, victims of meaningless home invasions or late-onset schizophrenia, lone suicides on solitary trips to the woods.

Those in control saw to it that there were no more questions, only redirected funds and areas of détente. An expanse of black-budget facilities, vehicles and men dangled from the normal government like a tumor—alien, but thriving despite the differences between it and the host. Eventually the tumor had infected enough of the host that it was in control; but death never came. Once it had the upper hand, using the secrets it had gained, equilibrium was established, and it faded into the background. The status quo had been fixed sometime back in the 1950s, Grant thought, back when the military ran the show. Now something scarier than the military was in control. Something stood behind the scenes and directed what it wanted, when it was wanted, and no one flinched. The wounds had long since scabbed over. The cancer had found a sweet spot and settled in.

Grant spent years guarding, protecting and carrying things he didn't really know much about except that he was told to stand between them and any threat. He was good at it. At first his imagination worked only when it was ordered to. Later, after the pieces of the puzzle slowly fell into place, he found it kept him up nights.

Then he met Lepus.

Over the four years that followed, the reality of his situation slowly spilled out, like a spreading stain, until it covered his whole life. His life before—the one that had seemed exciting and vibrant and full—was a lie, the same lie the group behind NRO DELTA had been feeding the world for decades. Madmen spoke of the military-industrial complex or some other secret group controlling the world—the Bilderbergers, the Illuminati, the Triumvirate—never knowing how close to the truth they actually were.

What did Grant know? What had he absorbed? He knew humanity wasn't alone. He knew there were other worlds with things plodding across the surface, building things, writing things, and reaching out into space. He knew that some had found their way here, across the great gaps between the stars. He knew they weren't friendly.

He knew that the Earth was at war and that only the group knew which way to point the missiles (there was no doubt that the group controlled them). He knew that the enemies—the Others—were small and grey and smelled like burning cardboard. He knew that humanity had nothing in its arsenal to match the weapons that the Greys' ships carried. He knew that they had us in check and there was nothing we could do now but squirm and search for some desperate ploy to escape.

Lepus told him the secrets, the most simple truths about the world that he and fewer than three hundred other people understood. Lepus showed him how to act, how to *be*. When the world was an illusion, when all the struggle and want and need on this Earth was nothing more than a flimsy distraction from the truth, only Lepus understood what to do.

Lepus knew what was what.

Eight months ago, Lepus let one more secret slide, on the sly. Justin Kroft—the leader of the group defending the Earth—had been turned.

It hadn't happened in the usual manner; there was no blackmail, no bribes. The aliens had insinuated themselves into Kroft through more invasive means. Early on, when America first forged a treaty with the Others, the aliens had given human scientists a few amazing books on Earthly genetics. At first, many thought these books would answer everything: Disease, even mortality could be rewritten. But there were problems. The hard facts of the universe remained: Change one thing and everything else shifts an infinitesimal amount. Change one protein to cure diabetes and the patient dies in agony as his skin hardens to stone. Shift one gene and the patient's limbs continue to grow until he dies of heart failure. The "Cookbook" was nothing more than a subtle trap. When the Others stopped communicating with the group and the treaty disintegrated, the Cookbook became useless.

Kroft, however, had continued the groups' research into the

Cookbook to meet his own ends. A hardened, nuclear-safeguarded biological containment and research facility in the Montana badlands, Facility-12, was where it was done. In the heyday of Cookbook research a handful of NRO DELTA agents had been modified in a project called ARC DREAM. Dozens died. Some came back disturbingly different. But they were just the appetizers for the main course.

Lepus had the tapes. Grant watched men writhe and die as their skin fell off, burst into flames or explode—or worse, become some sort of remote-controlled zombies.

One man Grant had known (hell, who had even covered his back in some nasty situations) volunteered for ARC DREAM. When his "treatment" was done, he calmly sat up from the examination table, stabbed a surgeon in the neck with a pair of scissors, and systematically killed every person in the room, one by one, with his hands. When he was done, the man broke into the computer system—and he had not been skilled with computers. After examining a series of seemingly unrelated files, he calmly cut his own throat with the automatic efficiency of tying his shoes.

The Others could do things like that. They could crawl in your head like a damp driver's seat and take you out on a fatal spin around the block.

The Cookbook let them in.

Eight months before Grant saw the last tape, Kroft had reclined on that table, surrounded by Facility-12 scientists who administered the treatment. Kroft had not exploded or died or killed anyone. He had sat up again and continued directing the group, as before. And he continued to receive treatments at Facility-12.

Lepus had told Grant that NRO DELTA was the last line of defense, that it was up to them to stem the tide. When the people who pulled the strings of NRO DELTA were themselves being controlled, could NRO DELTA comply with their demands? Wasn't it Lepus' and Grant's duty to stop such infiltration and corruption?

But first they needed to follow their movements, their plans, to learn the ideas that the Others were planting in their heads so they could be countered when the time came.

Grant suddenly found himself reassigned, in charge of Facility-12's security personnel.

For eight months he watched the changeling, Kroft, come and go. He obeyed its orders, protected it, waited for the moment when he would be told to eliminate the threat it represented.

Four hours ago, the order had come down. Eliminate Kroft and, if possible, Facility-12 itself.

Grant was the only man Lepus fully trusted. The other NRO DELTA agents would be a threat. It was up to him.

He would have to be quick.

FACILITY-12 WAS BUILT UNDERGROUND in a series of sealed hubs that surrounded a small nuclear warhead. For thirty years it had lived like a fat tick burrowed in the flesh of the Montana badlands. Scientists, money and specimens were poured in, and out came the dimmest outlines of alien science. The group sent debris from alien spacecraft, and alien creatures both alive and deceased, to Facility-12 for study and containment. The nuclear weapon was designed to be the final stage of containment, triggered automatically if any double-sealed rooms were opened on to each other at the same time. The weapon was large enough to carve a hole underneath the badlands the size of Shea Stadium if anything went wrong, but was small enough to escape immediate detection from the ground or air. Only Strategic Air Command, the Russians, and maybe the Chinese would know *definitively* that anything had gone wrong, if or when it did. Such detonations were not nearly as rare as the world imagined.

And Facility-12 knew there were things there that were best kept underground. But now, Grant knew, they were free and walking around. Hell, they were running the whole show.

He was standing next to one right now.

Grant, Kroft and four other NRO DELTA agents stood in the elevator as it descended to Facility-12, calmly regarding the matte beige of the doors. Kroft stood behind them; as usual he had met them at the airfield. They looked like attendants in some militant religious ritual. The NRO DELTA men held their weapons casually, unconcerned now that they were in a "safe" facility. Grant waited among them, his head humming with carefully devised plans waiting to be set in motion. He was giddy and eager. There was no fear. It was all clear in his mind.

At the base of the elevator shaft, nearly a mile down, was a hallway with two security men. When they arrived there would be a total of six men, then Kroft and himself. Tactically speaking, the hallway was a shooting gallery, which was both good and bad—bullets would be going both ways.

The elevator stopped and the men piled out but Grant hung back. Kroft approached the security desk of the narrow hallway and began the security protocols to enter. Grant removed a thermite grenade from his kit, pulled the pin, and tossed it into the elevator just as the doors swung closed. The fire protocols would be initiated once the building's systems detected the explosion and subsequent blaze.

By the time the firefight erupted, the elevator was a smoldering gap in the wall, lit from inside by a blinding blue-white light. Alarms sounded. NRO DELTA men scattered as Grant threw an anti-personnel grenade past the desk. The hallway shook with the detonation. Two DELTA agents remained, barely alive, and Kroft, looking ridiculously untouched, began to crawl away from the explosion. Towards Grant. He had no idea what was going on.

Grant had been hit four times by the time the second explosion erupted, but only two had missed his armor and drawn blood. Grant snatched up Kroft, throwing his arm around the man's chest. From the smoke, fire and alarms, he was met by silence. The gunfire stopped. Grant was almost completely obscured by Kroft's body, a human—or inhuman—shield. Shortly thereafter, the remaining DELTA men had retreated into the interior of the hallway, watching on the closed circuit.

Kroft began to whisper. Grant was sure it was unconscious.

"Oh my God, oh my God, stop, stop—"

Grant answered with the butt of his submachine gun to the back of his head.

Incredibly, an intercom sprang to life, barely audible over the ringing in his ears.

"Orders, sir?" Grant didn't need to ask who they were talking to.

Grant pushed the MP5 into the back of Kroft's skull and said, "Tell them to do anything I say."

"Do anything he says, do anything he says," Kroft parroted. "What do you want?"

"Failsafe codes," Grant murmured.

"What? But—" Kroft shouted wildly.

Grant dug the barrel deeper into Kroft's thin hair.

Grant punched a twelve-digit number into the console from memory. His code. Two matching codes were necessary for the failsafe to fire.

"That'll kill us all. Nuclear safeguard, I can't—"

"I can make this last a long time, or it can be over in a second. Your choice." Grant's finger put a pound of force on the trigger of the submachine gun; one more, and there would be a mess. Kroft, freed, immediately collapsed to the ground on his hands and knees.

Grant's MP5 tracked his back. Only blood, spent shell casings and some unidentified burned limb were in Kroft's view. He tried to weep, but all he felt was an endless looping terror that ran over and over again through his mind like a nonsensical tune.

Kroft struggled to his feet and, swaying, entered two numbers on the console. Each number entered seemed to take seconds. For a moment Grant wasn't sure if he was going to finish, but when the number sequence went red, Grant sighed.

The alarms took on a new, more drastic tone.

"Just what do you think you're accomplishing here?" Kroft said quietly, with something like resignation in his voice, hands behind his head like a hostage. But Grant knew it was a monster, the monster in control of the whole show.

Grant smiled as the countdown began over the intercom, an antiseptic voice reading off numbers that measured all the time they had left.

"I'm saving the world."

Grant realized, then, that if the weapon was the safeguard for the facility, he was the safeguard for the group. He was the weapon. The device timed to prevent the worst possible outcome from occurring.

"I'm saving the world," he said again, quieter and more sure of himself.

"I'm saving the world from you."

It was the last thing either of them ever heard.

Stimulus/Response

Second police interview in the disappearance of Robert M. Lumsden: New Brunswick, New Jersey. 40.48 N/74.46 W latitude/longitude. Approximately 1,224 miles from Facility-12: Friday, February 9, 2001, 1:00 P.M. EST.

IN THE HALL OF the New Brunswick Police Department, Detective Aaron Orville paused, each hand holding a cup full of water. The feeling would not leave him. He tested it again, and again something rose from the depths, a warning. Inside Interview Room Four, less than twenty feet away, his partner Detective Grogan was questioning their chief suspect in the Robert Lumsden disappearance, Vincent Garrity. Garrity was an egghead, someone who would not usually raise any alarm in the solidly built Orville. The suspect had to pass through two metal detectors to get to the interview, after all; he wasn't packing. He was big, true, but it was nothing a Glock couldn't put in order. Besides, he didn't feel dangerous, exactly. It was something else. Something deeper.

Orville downed a cup of water. His face was a blank, looking emptily down the abandoned hallway. It was lunch, so no one was here; the place was a ghost town. They had brought Garrity in at this time for a reason, but what that reason was he now couldn't recall. This bugged him as well. Without his expression changing, Orville crumpled the paper cup and tossed it at the waste basket under the bulletin board. It landed on top of the endless pile of crushed cups, momentarily vanishing in their sameness, and then slowly slid off onto the floor, becoming unique again.

All at once animation returned to him, like someone had flipped a switch. Orville opened the door next to Interview 4 and stepped into the dark closet with the two-way mirror, quietly closing the door behind him. A video camera on a tripod hummed away in the dark, its lens occasionally making a nearly imperceptible buzzing noise as it auto-focused on the subjects in the room. Past the mirror, Vincent Garrity sat calmly across from Detective Grogan.

"So, Vince, what have you been up to?" Grogan asked.

Detective Orville considered Vincent Garrity from behind the mirror like someone studying a painting. He moved his blunt face up until it was a half-inch from the glass and his breath fogged it in two sloping wings of condensation. All this had happened before. Questions, responses, vague accusations, denials. This was the second time they had hauled in the young scientist—but something about it, some vital thing was different. It hung in the air like a bad smell he couldn't place.

It was fine when they had picked him up in the cruiser. Garrity had climbed in without protest, making a slight, self-deprecating wave as they pulled up to his condominium. The ride had been pleasant, with talk focusing mostly on local sports. Finally, Grogan had turned on Z100 and they had settled into a silence overshadowed by the music.

It had all been fine in the car.

They arrived, trundled out, and went up to the second floor in the elevator in silence. Something had struck a chord the moment the suspect sat down, a warning, a tone in the back of Orville's head that raised his heart rate and made his hackles stand up. *Goddamnit, something is* different *about him*, he thought. Orville's mind turned the problem over and over like a puzzle box with no seams; his mind couldn't find a split in the surface, that lip that might gain him entry. It was smooth. A puzzle without any possible answer. But the feeling was there.

Some secret thing, as Orville looked, seemed to belong somewhere on Garrity's person. *Was* Garrity's person. He got as far as that and then lost the thread again. He banked on feelings like this.

His job depended on a level of observation at least a step above the norm, and he felt like he had that special something which made good detectives great. In any case, he wouldn't find it here behind the glass.

He took the second door into the interview room and sat down, sliding a cup of water over to Garrity. Vincent Garrity lifted the cup, smiled, and then downed it.

Grogan, his partner, sat next to him, unperturbed; it was clear to Orville that Grogan didn't see it—whatever "it" was.

Grogan was on the same old tack. He was plying Garrity for answers on a dozen small, seemingly insignificant facts, hoping to catch him in a lie. Garrity was smarter than both of them put together. They knew that. But that wasn't a big deal. There had been many times when the guy on the far side of the table was smarter than either of them, and that fact alone could cause a slip-up. Smart people loved to talk. They loved to extrapolate. They loved to embellish. They told their stories in lazy loops until the detectives had enough slack to pull it taut and catch them. Garrity, however, was elusive.

Finally, Orville couldn't take it anymore. He knew he was doing the detective equivalent of dropping his pants, but he didn't care. He needed to know.

"Hey, Vince," Orville began, "is there something—different about you?"

Grogan coughed and looked over at Orville, as if to say, *What the fuck are you doing?*

Garrity seemed to absorb this question as Orville studied him. He was really not the kind of guy who turned up when you gave a shake to the principals involved in this kind of disappearance. They were usually ex-girlfriends, ex-husbands, people with a grudge or something financial to gain. He knew Garrity had no worries in the money department. Lumsden wasn't a threat to him in any way they could place; but still, Garrity's name was the only one which sounded when they lined up the facts.

Garrity was big, but not overweight—he looked fit, neither too muscular nor too fat. His frame was a perfect V, topped by a handsome, bored-looking face. His deep-set blue eyes examined the room in a cool gaze. Above them curly brown locks in a perfect, Caesar-like haircut somehow looked carefully maintained and a bit tousled at the same time. Garrity had it all. He was brilliant and handsome and rich. The looks and brains were a genetic crap-shoot, and Garrity had rolled well. The money—well, he had made it in the last ten years with a few small investments snowballing into monstrous bankrolls. Orville supposed that, too, was because of his brains and genetics. The guy was set. There was no motive for him to go after Lumsden.

"I gotta say, Detective Orville, you are really very good. I am really, really impressed," Garrity finally said, his face split by a shy, retiring smile. He threw his hands up as if to say, *You got me.* Grogan cleared his throat.

"So, um—Vince. What's changed?"

Grogan coughed.

Garrity put his hands flat on the table and smiled. The room seemed to pause for a moment.

"I am now in control of all things," Garrity said with a smirk.

"Oh," Grogan responded, without thinking.

He pushed his chair back and gave a glance over at Orville which said, *He's fucking lost it.* Orville didn't have to look to know Grogan was doing this; they had been partners for six years. Orville's eyes did not leave Garrity's face. There was something behind the eyes that looked serene, even bored. Bored with the whole world. As if he had not only seen it all before, but had created it.

They both waited for Garrity to continue speaking, to move, to do something, but the only real lead they had just sat there, smiling calmly. He had not been calm the last time, Orville thought suddenly. A picture arrived in Orville's mind clearly, as if it had risen, whole-cloth, from nothingness. It was not a memory but something else. A fragment floating in the void of his mind, suddenly connected to a conscious thought which rose up in his mind's eye. In it, a sweaty, fat man squatted in the chair now occupied by Garrity.

It seemed terribly important, but it meant nothing to Orville.

"Vince, this is really not appropriate," Orville finally said. "This is a very serious situation."

"For you, sure, yeah, it's pretty serious," Garrity agreed.

"What does that mean?" Grogan said.

Garrity folded his hands and leaned forward.

"I mean, if I tell you this, you're not going to believe it, but that won't really matter, either."

"So, then. . . ."

Garrity seemed to think it over and then finally, with a shrug, spoke.

"What if I told you I'm going to erase both of you from existence?"

It took a few seconds for the words to sink in.

"Is that a threat?" Grogan said, his eyebrows coming down. "Because threatening a police officer is a felony, Mr. Garrity."

Garrity laughed.

"No, no threat. I'm going to do it."

Grogan stood up then and took a step back, but something wouldn't let Orville rise as well. There was something in Garrity's demeanor, his voice, his face, which seemed to grab the room and all of its contents in an iron grasp. Grogan's hand found his gun-butt at his belt and he stood, pushing his chair back with a groan of wood on rubber.

"Stand up," Grogan ordered, pointing a finger at Garrity's chest.

"You are pretty damn exceptional for a human, Detective Orville," Garrity continued. He ignored Grogan, staring only into Orville's face.

Orville was expecting another command from Grogan—"On your feet," or perhaps "You're under arrest"—but nothing came. There was no sound of a gun coming out of its holster, no jingle of handcuffs, no requests for assistance.

"Now that we're alone," Garrity said, "I think I'll reward your unique abilities of observation with something not many people who interfere with me get to see."

Again, it took a few seconds for this to sink in. Orville finally turned his head to find the room empty except for Garrity and himself. There was no Grogan, only a vacant chair turned out a little bit, as if someone had sat in it but had stood in a hurry.

Orville found he couldn't speak.

"If you looked, now—and you'll have to take my word for it—neither you nor Detective Grogan exist. I've wiped the slate clean. Gone back a generation and cleared up the blemishes on my life called 'Grogan' and 'Orville.' I've left you here, because, well, you actually noticed a change, and that makes you special."

Orville swallowed and considered his gun, but Garrity laughed even before Orville knew he was going to look at it. That laugh said, *Go ahead, pull your gun and see what happens.* Orville found his mind stuttering on the single fact that Grogan was gone. His thoughts butted up against this impossibility and rolled back. No forward progress was possible.

"Your mother Eileen never had a child. Detective Grogan's mother died a year before he was born."

At the sound of his mother's name, Orville's heart began jackhammering in his chest.

"My kids——" Orville said.

"What kids? You don't exist," Garrity said somberly. "How can you have any kids?"

Orville heard someone emit one huge sob, something so deep and real that it took him a moment to realize the sound had emanated from his own mouth. He clapped his hands to his mouth, which seemed to want to open wider and wider—expanding, he imagined, until his head split down the middle and dropped off to roll on the floor.

"So, anyway, before you go, I'll solve your case for you. Bob Lumsden's like me. He's beyond all of this. Trust me, he's not in some shallow grave somewhere. I didn't kill him. I'm not even sure I could kill him."

Orville mustered all he was to remove his hands from his mouth. There was spit all over the lower half of his face which stretched in thin transparent strings to his fingertips. He struggled to speak.

"The machine," Orville said.

"You really are very good. You are exactly right. The machine. In any case, goodbye, Detective Orville."

"Goodbye," Orville found himself saying.

But then, no one had been in the room, no one had picked up Garrity, no one had phoned him up or investigated the disappearance at all. The last loop in the problem had been unravelled, and the string of causality was a straight unbroken line again.

Garrity, observing this all, considered his work and then went elsewhere.

Kept Men

Ross hits a wall: Mount Weather, Virginia. 38.98 N/76.50 W latitude/ longitude. Approximately 154 miles from New Brunswick, New Jersey: Saturday, February 10, 2001, 1:01 A.M. EST.

WORD CAME DOWN THE wire that Kroft had evaporated in the badlands of Montana at 1456. By 1500 Ross, barely conscious, was on the move. A contingent of twenty-seven men gathered him, his papers, a few hard drives, and not much else, hoping to flee before Lepus could regroup and move in for the kill.

The phone rang once in the dark before Ross picked it up and, eyes closed, connected it to his ear. The voice rattled off the information, the statement that everything MAJESTIC had—all its personnel and facilities and its huge budget—were in play. The facts didn't really register with Ross as they were said.

Things happened quickly after that.

The security door beeped open, revealing a hallway lit by supernova, broken by hulking shadows clanking with combat gear, the plastic and metal sounds of modern weaponry. Rough arms hoisted him from his bed before he could wipe the sleep from his eyes. The phone was dropped and left on the meticulously clean, cream shag carpet.

Barefoot and half-awake in a pair of Bergdorf Goodman pajamas, Ross was walked like a dog, led by somber-faced men who brimmed with explosives and weaponry through the endless beige halls of the Country Club. Despite the obvious sense of danger, the dullness would not leave his mind. It was like watching a film, a tedious, boring film that failed, in a million ways, to rouse his interest. Now that this moment—his death—had finally arrived, he found he just didn't care.

A left, a right, stairs, stairs, security door, security door, and finally an enclosed garage with eight black 4x4s, idling, filled with MAJESTIC's secrets. Ross settled into the back of a truck and, heavy-lidded, considered the shadows outside. Men shouted orders, splitting into careful groups, settling into long preordained roles. It was hard to believe this was a dream. Things were too orderly, too precise.

Within seconds, they were ready. The door to the garage rose quickly and silently, revealing a drenched darkness beyond. In the circle of lights which cut the night open, rain pelted the perfect asphalt. Beyond that there was only void.

Even this efficiency and firepower didn't particularly mean anything; they were still surrounded on all sides by NRO DELTA. The Country Club was a deathtrap filled with eager killers, all hoping to climb Lepus' totem pole on top of Ross' corpse. The extraction had been planned in detail some time before, but Ross never considered the possibility of a coup with Lepus at its head. Kroft had been too monolithic to ever consider him simply vanishing in one night.

But Kroft was gone. Coffey was gone. That left just Ross and Lepus, and Lepus would not hesitate. The rest of the Steering Committee didn't matter. Not anymore. They were sheep—followers despite all their rank—accustomed to leadership. The trucks slowed as they drifted to the east gate, nothing more than a spluttery white light outside the tinted windows. When the gate came up, they drove into the dark.

MT. WEATHER WAS A vast facility only fifty miles from the seat of the U.S. government. Overground it was a series of reinforced bunkers, garages, helipads and winding roads, covered in forest and filled with a natural beauty which belied the fact that it was a tiny, underground version of Washington D.C. Thousands of rooms, hallways, galleries, storage facilities and more crowded together there beneath the

Blue Ridge Mountains, maintained by anonymous crews awaiting the end of the world and the beginning of their work.

In case of nuclear attack, Mt. Weather was where most of the civilian government would be evacuated. The President would be moved elsewhere. It was easy for MAJESTIC to do as they wished there. In the earliest days of the group, portions of what would become the Country Club were built at Mt. Weather while the civilian facility was constructed in tandem. The two were connected, in limited ways, and those in command of the facility were in MAJESTIC's control. The endless black budget which poured into Mt. Weather was never questioned.

By the mid-1980s, Mt. Weather comprised nearly 1,600,000 square feet of underground facilities, only 600,000 of which were acknowledged in budgets and reports. The remaining 1,000,000 square feet represented the command post of MAJESTIC—the Country Club.

To those who worked in the "official" half, the rest of the facility was off-limits. The scuttlebutt alternatively identified this secondary area as an NSA data vault, a place which stored secret U.S. gold reserves, or a private playground for the rich and powerful. In truth, it was a mix of all of those things.

In the dark, on the winding roads which crisscrossed Mt. Weather, it was easy to get lost. Crews that worked there preferred the clearly marked tunnels beneath the mountain to the roads above. Even in full daylight they were confusing.

Despite the number of people packed underground, you could drive a long time up top without seeing anything or anyone at all.

Ross had no idea where he was. He was used to entering the facility by helicopter, and had only been driven in once, and then in full daylight. In the truck, nameless curving roads spun off into an infinite blackness spotted with a grey rain. He could only sit back and wait.

The 4x4 stopped suddenly and randomly. From his vantage point, Ross could see nothing to stop for, and before he could reorient himself to see, the door was flung open and he was pulled roughly from the vehicle. As he attempted to find his balance on the freezing, wet ground, the truck sped off into the dark.

An implacable hand clutched at Ross' arm, an inch or two too high to be comfortable, and bent his arm at an angle that made lack of forward motion impossible. His feet seemed to move on their own, flapping dully on the wet pavement.

Ross heard a helicopter spinning up and suddenly found himself pulled in that direction in a stumbling, numb-footed march. The black hole of the door of the chopper bounced in his vision as the contingent of men pushed him forward.

The whine of the rotors masked the suppressed shots, but they were visible as blue-white pops of light in the dark of the door. The man next to Ross was caught high in the neck, and Ross was sprayed by hot blood as the carotid artery let go. By the time he realized fully what was happening—that they were being fired upon from inside the helicopter—all the men with him were dead, sprawled on the ground in poses that would have been comedic in any other situation.

Ross stood, freezing, shaken in the rain—he was not dead. The rotors spun down as he attempted to make sense of the situation. Four men in combat gear hopped from the helicopter with their guns trained on the field. One man touched an ear and said something. One man put a round into each of the men next to Ross at close range, and each time the weapon fired with its dry, clanking sound, Ross jumped. Two men swung in behind Ross.

Were they NRO DELTA?

Ross tried to puff himself up as much as he could, but in the rain, in the dark, he didn't think it was very effective.

"Gavin Ross, MJ-3," he said. "I'm instituting an emergency lockdown protocol."

The man who Ross pegged as the leader began hunting through Ross' pockets, ignoring him. Ross kept his posture, refusing to cooperate.

"Hands at the head, sir," he said in a voice laced with Southern undertones.

"I'm in command here!" Ross slapped the man's hand from him.

The commando leaned in close to Ross and smiled. Ross easily had two inches on him, but the man talked to him like one might talk to a child. His teeth were perfect and startlingly white.

"Don't do that again." The voice was implacable. The commando went back to his search. Wouldn't Lepus just put a bounty on him? Wouldn't they just gun him down here? Ross decided to test the situation. So far, it seemed that an odd sort of luck was on his side.

"Stand down," Ross shouted, and swatted the man's hand away again.

The man reached for his sidearm and for a split second, Ross thought he had stepped over the last line, before the man shucked the action, caught the bullet in the air, and returned his firearm to the holster. Grabbing Ross' hand roughly, the commando pressed the round into his palm. It was cold and solid.

"Put that in your pocket. The next time you touch me, sir, I will beat you, take that bullet from you, and put it in your brain." The man was no longer smiling. Ross had made a career of reading intentions. This man was not bluffing.

Ross put his hands to his head and tried not to show any fear. It was very, very hard.

Δ

FINALLY THEY STOOD IN front of a small, squat, cinder-block building with a curved steel roof. It looked like one of the ventilation shafts that dotted the mountain. BLOCK 4, the painted legend on the cement read.

The door opened from within. Ross was shoved inside and followed by two men. The door slammed with a bang and a beep.

"Who is in command of your unit?" Ross said, turning now that they were inside. He came face to face with the open maw of a submachine gun held just above the tip of his nose. He stared down the barrel and everything seemed to slow. He could hear his heartbeat in his chest, could feel it, as his eyes sank into the black of the barrel. Tiny grooves were filagreed there, highlights of silver disappearing into the dark. When they pulled the bullet from his skull, he thought, they could see those lines etched in reverse on the slug like a signature.

"You get one more pass, just because the boss likes you. After that, you were shot trying to escape. Or maybe you tried to grab my weapon," the voice behind the submachine gun said. A mild voice. The voice of a banker. Tens or twenties. It was everyday, boring. The voice said that Ross' death was merely an inconvenience, more paperwork. Nothing more.

There was a very audible click of the safety being switched off.

Ross had done this—ordered this exact thing—a hundred, a thousand times, and he was conscious that his bladder had let go, but no one else seemed to pay any attention. His pajamas darkened at his waist. A wet, slapping noise filled the room as the urine hit the ground at his feet, further soaking them. The smell wafted upwards. The men didn't react, didn't laugh, they just quietly returned to their business.

Two other men guarded an inner door and Ross was marched through at a brisk pace. The lock was operated by hand-scan and card. With a ding, the door opened and Ross was shuffled down an anonymous hallway. He was sent through another door and heard it locked behind him with a series of bolts that put him in mind of old prison movies. He was in what looked like one of the civilian quarters for dignitaries forced to ground by a national emergency. A grey room, a simple bed, a sink and a toilet. Two dull steel wardrobes.

A cell.

Alone, but certain he was being watched, Ross stood still at the door, shaking, smelling of piss and fear. His hands were still at his head. Waiting for Lepus, waiting for the bullet, waiting for interrogation and torture. It felt like hours, but only ten minutes passed.

Finally, just as he brought his arms down, the door opened.

Forrest James stepped in.

Ross' face collapsed as several emotions crawled across it in waves: joy, relief, exhaustion. But James didn't react. The man stepped into the room, owning it, and pointed at a chair.

"James, thank God. I need—some new clothing. . . ."

In response, James pointed at the chair once again. His face did not change.

Shaking, Ross sat down.

"NRO DELTA is locked down, but Lepus and nearly ninety of his men are still on the loose," James finally said.

"The VIPs?" Ross asked.

"I have Bostick, Yrjo and most of the others," James responded.

"How?"

"Same way I got you. We have all the evacuation orders. Up until about ten minutes ago, NRO DELTA was still calling in BLUE FLY for air support. My copters brought them in and took them out. It was easy to take control when they were in the air and we knew where they were going. Of course, now they're aware that we're trying to shut them down, so. . . ."

Ross put his face in his hands. His chest felt too tight. His head was swimming.

"Listen," James began, and then considered himself very carefully. He continued:

"I'm assuming command. The focus of the group has been lost. The old guard can't be trusted. Lepus needs to be eliminated. The group needs to get back to doing what it was created for— protecting the American people."

Ross looked up, his face flushed and his eyes bloodshot. His first thought was to shout, to scream, to rip into James like he had done a hundred times before. In his mind, the million elements he had lined up, that he had meticulously assembled into a seamless bastion of personal power, began to shake, began to crack. He shook this feeling off like a fighter ducking a punch.

Instead of overreacting, Ross pictured the barrel of the submachine gun in his face, the ease with which its wielder had expressed the concept of Ross' death.

What was the play? What could he say or do to reverse this—or failing that, to buy time?

"I see," Ross replied.

"You're going to help me," James continued.

Ross knew then that James needed him. There was something behind his eyes, a proprietary fear, like a man who doesn't know his own house, one that he has just inherited, a valuable home, perhaps the most valuable in the world, but a haunted house all the same. There were things Ross knew, and that James knew he knew, which could push back the darkness. As long as that utility existed, as long as Ross could drag that out, he was too valuable to liquidate. And in that time, there was the possibility of regaining control, of escape.

"If that's what you want, Forrest," Ross responded calmly.

"You are a smart man, Gavin. At one time, your eye was on the prize. You brought me in, you showed me what was going on. I haven't forgotten that." James looked almost sad.

Ross recalled reading James' psychological evaluation two years before: *Subject operates on what he imagines to be a higher level of morality than the rank and file. Artificially clear sense of "justice." Utilized properly, can become a zealot for the project. Dangerous if betrayed.*

"You're going to stay here," James said. "You're going to answer the questions put to you. You're going to help me put this all in order so we can keep the world spinning or—you won't."

Ross opened his mouth, but reconsidered and closed it again. That was the play: Kept man. Consigliere at gunpoint. If he could prove himself, if he could buy some trust, maybe, just maybe he would see freedom again. And then he could deal with James. Until then, it was his job to be a servant, and a humble one at that. He had not ascended to the top of the most powerful conspiracy on the Earth by being a fool.

"If I hear you attempting to recruit my personnel," James said, "if I find you trying to escape, if I discover even one shred of evidence that you are planning a move against me, they'll march you upstairs and cut you in half."

Ross, eyes unblinking and wide, nodded once. *You are in control,* that look said.

"It will help to have you, Gavin, but I don't *need* you. Don't forget that," James said. Turning, he looked at the camera in the upper right hand corner and announced he was coming out.

James exited and the recessed bolts in the door slid shut with a clang.

We'll see who needs whom in the end, Ross thought, and began to change his clothing. He found a pair of plastic-sealed flannel pajamas—placed in the locker sometime in the late 1970s, by the style—stripped his soaked clothing and slipped them on. They felt warm. He could be comfortable here, now that he knew James was in command. Now that he knew he was needed. Now that he knew he had time.

He felt like a man who had meticulously mapped the world around him until every city, every road, every corner, was known to him, only to wake unexpectedly in a new strange world, a world without map and compass. Here he would have to move and stop when the world willed it; he was no longer its master. He would have to pay attention to the new, unexplored ground. He would have to be clever. Or he would have to die.

Sitting at the small steel desk considering his options sometime later, he surprised himself. He was smiling.

SOMEWHERE A MILE TO east, and nearly five hundred feet underground, Charles Bostick sat uncomfortably in an observation room in front of his laptop. He was confused, and scared, but no longer as scared as he had once been. Something big was going on, that much was obvious.

Stepping off the chopper at the Country Club had been the *second* most harrowing experience in his life. At least no one was pointing guns at him.

The goons had offloaded him from the transport helicopter in the dark, in the midst of a persistent, freezing drizzle which coated his glasses and faded everything to a blurry, water-soaked grey. As the helicopter lifted off again and disappeared, and the group crossed the open space to the entry checkpoint, the man holding his arm had suddenly tightened his grip. Bostick, who was resigned to his shuffling fate, felt the grip tighten and then close on his skinny arm like a vise, pulling him backwards.

"Hey!" Bostick shouted, and yanked hard, pulling his arm free. It was only then he realized all four men with him were lying on the ground. He stood, frozen in place, in the whipping rain, surrounded on all sides by corpses, the only man left standing on the field.

For several seconds, Bostick goggled at what had gone on in between the moments he was paying attention. There was no sound but the wind and the rain, a persistent chatter.

Bostick considered the bodies on the ground. One man, the one who had laughed so readily at him in the hotel room when he had shit himself, had a single, black smoking hole just below his eye, above the bone but below the eyeball. As Bostick watched, black, shining liquid began to fill upwards from that hole, covering his blank eye in blood and sliding off his upturned face. Soon, that black crept out onto the grey tarmac in a spreading pool.

"Oh!" Bostick exclaimed. "Shit, shit, shit—" the words seemed to drop from his mouth on their own, each dragging the next with it. Shot. They had been shot. He stepped forward, ready to run, and then hesitated and put his hands up in the air in a comedic parody of surrender, his coat bunched at his shoulders and rose up the back of his neck, until he looked like a terrified turtle, eyes wide and full of fear.

"Hey! Charles Bostick! Analyst! I'm not with these . . . assholes!"

Men appeared. A dozen or more, sweeping the field with guns, ready for any possible target. Two approached Bostick with their guns leveled at the men on the ground. They seemed more interested in the corpses than in Bostick himself. The rest swung into a loose circle around him.

"Whoah! Hey! I'm Charles Bo—"

"We know who you are, sir, and we're here to protect you," the man in the lead, nothing more than a plain-faced killer in a deep blue combat suit, said. Then slinging his weapon he placed his hand on his ear.

"BLUE FLY 2, A-2, we have the package, Field 4 secure."

The guns were turned out pointed into the dark. The BLUE FLY commander laid his hand on Bostick's back in a gesture which said, *Excuse me.*

"If you'll come with us sir, we're in lockdown. We need to get you inside."

Bostick followed, and only a moment or two into his walk realized his arms were still up.

And now he had been here, in this room, for four hours. Food had been brought, as had his laptop (with its intranet protocols disabled, he noted), but no one had spoken more than a dozen words to him. The men who came and exited were BLUE FLY, and for that, he was profoundly grateful; they were trained killers, but in comparison to the NRO DELTA psychos the BLUE FLY men were like waiters. Calm, quiet and polite. They wore guns, yes, but Bostick never felt threatened by them. In fact, he was fairly certain they had saved his life.

He wondered who would open that door when it was time to talk. Couldn't be Lepus. Maybe Ross had stepped up, finally taking Kroft out? One of the others. Unlikely. He didn't know who had made the play, but he knew why, or at least he thought he knew why.

The God Box. They had found out about the God Box. Nothing short of that could put a series of wild exchanges in play except something so potentially earth-shattering as to change the disposition of everything.

The God Box.

What command *didn't* know—or at least he *thought* they didn't know—was that Bostick had the plans for the God Box, the program that ran it and more. He had everything short of the device itself, but that could be recreated. The plans had been easy to get—Garrity was a meticulous inventor, eager to protect his creation, and the documents that he filed with the U.S. Patent Office had been well detailed. NRO DELTA men had copied and deleted the software from the university system, and from every laptop, disk and external hard drive they could find, two hours before he had touched down in New Brunswick. The only other people who knew any of this were going cold on the tarmac somewhere up in the dark. But even they hadn't known what the plans and the software really meant.

Was there anyone who could come through that door who could be trusted with such a thing?

Who would come through that door?

Bostick, bored with the questions rolling in his mind, opened his laptop, launched Minesweeper and started to play another round.

Devil, Details

Charlie does some homework: Hotel Dreyfus, Philadelphia, Pennsylvania. 39.93 N/75.18 W latitude/longitude. Approximately 109 miles from the "Country Club": Sunday, February 11, 2001, 1:06 P.M. EST.

DONALD POE COULD NEVER be accused of being a subtle man. He was as straightforward as a bone mallet, an implement fashioned by a million different decisions for a specific purpose. He got the job done. He never asked questions. That's why he had lasted so long.

He considered these facts while he set up his sniper's nest. He was a soldier. He had a mission.

But the doubt wouldn't leave his mind.

Why are they giving up Lepus? What does it gain them?

The question would not go away. It sat in the back of his mind, like something caught in his teeth, rising up from the dark whenever he ceased thinking about how to move forward. He tried to keep his mind on the task at hand, tried to busy himself with the million different things he needed to guarantee a perfect shot.

He had scouted the area out in a twenty-five minute period on foot, trotting in a loose semi-circle around the small metropolitan hotel where Lepus was supposedly staying. Poe spotted the NRO DELTA goons without even trying. Two on the front entrance, two more at a 4x4, more inside. Men in nondescript suits poised with the swagger of the select few. They wore shoulder rigs with dump holsters, slow, clumsy things. Poe felt something for them—an affinity, maybe. But the more he thought about it, he thought maybe it was more like pity. They thought they were on top, but they were just lapdogs. All lapdogs think they're on top until it's too late.

A lot of them would die. Maybe a lot of innocents, too. He understood this was the price he would pay to have Lepus. Nothing came for free, and to kill the devil you had to lose something—maybe even your soul—in the process. Everyone knew that.

But he was getting ahead of himself.

The fact that NRO DELTA was present meant nothing by itself. Looking at the secure tracking website, this seemed to be Lepus' base of operations: a nondescript hotel in Philadelphia. For nine hours out of the last sixteen, Lepus had been here, in room 5A, guarded around the clock. When he moved, an entourage fell in around him—cars and men and weapons. Right here, right in the heart of Philadelphia.

Philadelphia. The city which had mobilized the entirety of its law enforcement to look for Donald Poe. Here he was with a .50 caliber sniper rifle set up on a rooftop of a parking garage, dead center in the middle of the dragnet tasked with capturing him. If only the mayor, the chief of police, and the head of the federal task force could see him now. Poe imagined the scene, all three lined up on the roof, watching him peer down the scope, powerless while he prepared to rain a clip of half-pound slugs on a hotel filled with innocents. In fact, this would be his second hotel in as many weeks. Poe cracked his knuckles and grimaced.

He honestly couldn't say he regretted any action he had taken. He wasn't sure if that made him insane or just good at what he did. Or if there was even a difference.

He slowly assumed the firing position, like an old man who had strained his back. He was solid, and still strong despite his age, but time had taken its toll. The huge rifle was set up on the rooftop of the elevator port on the concrete roof, tucked underneath the triangle overhang which kept the water off, invisible from the street and even invisible from the air, unless they were searching for him. The roof was unused, which is why he had chosen it. It held a sea of long-term parkers, cars left unattended for months while their owners did who-knows-what.

From here he had overwatch on the entire north side of the hotel, and as he settled in and squinted to peer through the scope, the world a half-mile away jumped into focus. Bricks, a patio door, vines crawling up a wall in vivid, drastic detail. Birds, a snaking grey wire roughly stapled to the stucco, and finally the room. He knew it was the room because a secure phone box sat on the window-side table.

He had seen one before—stolen it, in fact—in Groversville.

He shrugged off a chill.

He looked away, stroked the trigger with several time-worn nervous habits, and gave it three pounds of its five-pound pull. He settled his eye into the scope again and the world a half-mile away swung into focus: a stucco wall of ivy, a lamp jutting from the corner of the hotel like a rotted tooth, a window frame. He shifted with his finger still held down on the trigger, and counted up and across to Lepus' suite.

A figure was in the window.

Poe's heart leapt into his chest. A thousand ideas spilled through his mind at that moment. A helicopter ambush, men pouring from vans laden with assault gear, a counter-sniper team taking bead on his head like a fresh, untouched melon, Lepus throwing open the window and exploding in a spray of blood and gristle.

But as the silence spun out, Poe regained control. The figure was not Lepus. It was an old man, an old man known to Poe. The yellowed eyes, the hunched form projected all of its years out at him. The tired old man watched Poe—his eyes were a piercing deep blue and they looked directly at him. They looked at Poe with a clear and absolute knowledge of his location and intention. The figure was somber and certain.

Despite himself, Poe's crosshairs found the figure's center mass and settled there.

It took all his power not to pull the trigger.

The old man shook his head once; a no go. Then, he faded as if the room itself had swallowed him. Within seconds, he was gone. Poe was staring down the barrel at an empty room.

Without looking back, Donald Poe struggled to his feet, turned and fled the parking garage as if he was pursued by ghosts.

Later, Poe sat in his nondescript car in Philadelphia with both huge arms outstretched, clutching the steering wheel as if it were the only thing that held him to the Earth. Something was playing with his life like a cat plays with an injured mouse. He had known for years—decades—that the world was a puzzle built of secrets, but he thought the things that haunted the edges of human knowledge were nothing more than mindless beings bent on destruction and chaos.

The idea that his life was some sort of toy to one of these things was unacceptable. His mind balked at the concept. It was wrong. No matter how he tried to feature it, he couldn't choke it down. But the man at the window. That man. That man had sent him around the world fighting those things. How could he be there? How did he—it—leave?

He dropped the car into gear and drove off.

WHEN McRAY WOKE, HE found the hulking form of Poe sitting in an ancient formica chair. Poe was hunched over, his hands clasped together between his knees, clutching a huge pistol.

McRay felt weak and far away. He tried to speak once, twice, and then finally managed to croak a question.

"So?"

Poe looked up slowly. What McRay saw there frightened him deeply. Poe's eyes were bloodshot and puffy. His face was pale and empty of any clear emotion. Even through the dull pain which filled McRay's body, this fact—Poe had been crying—drilled through to the deepest portion of his mind. It cleared the clouds of pain away from his thoughts for the first time.

"Hey," Poe said. "We're out of here. I've got a place. We need to get out of the city." Poe wiped his nose and eyes.

"Lepus," McRay muttered. "Did you get him?"

Poe looked back down at his gun. There was silence for a long time. So long that McRay faded out, and was brought back around only by Poe's response.

"Something's got him."

Target

Lepus feels something: Hotel Dreyfus, Philadelphia, Pennsylvania. 39.93 N/75.18 W latitude/longitude. Approximately nine miles from Interstate 95: Monday, February 12, 2001, 5:05 A.M. EST.

WHEN THE PHONE RANG, Lepus started awake, reached for his gun, and holstered it. He knew who was on the line. Neither one of them was in a rush. He could take his time.

As the phone rang again, he placed both hands flat on his face and breathed through his fingers, feeling his pale face warmed by his breath.

He rested his hand on the phone on the third ring.

"Don't you sleep, old man?" Lepus finally said into the receiver, attempting to sound as if he had been waiting next to the phone since their last meeting, awake. In actuality he had slept a lot in the last few days, his nights wracked by forgotten, dark dreams. The dreams were soupy and indistinct, and vanished like smoke when he tried to grasp them. A light, the jungle. Screaming.

He didn't try to recall it.

Joe Camp was silent on the other end of the line except for low, labored breathing. Lepus waited. He had time. Kroft was gone, Ross was on the run, Coffey was dead. Things had gone south at the Country Club; some fuck from BLUE FLY had stepped up. But it didn't matter. It was only a matter of time.

"I've got Poe's location if you want it."

Something jumped in Lepus at the mention of the name, and he sat up. He had expected Camp to crawfish on their deal after he eliminated Kroft. The old man was stupid; hell, Lepus was going to do Kroft anyway. But just the fact that the old man was on the phone told Lepus he was going to follow through.

Or set him up. But so many people had tried that trick before.

"Go ahead."

Camp spilled out coordinates. Lepus wrote them on his palm with a marker.

"A cabin. He's gone to ground. He's heavily armed."

"Yeah? Hey, Camp?"

Silence.

Lepus said, "After him, I'll be seeing you."

"I'll be waiting."

Lepus hung up.

THE BLACK HAWKS WERE waiting at Andrews. The day was overcast and dreary as the 4x4s tore across the airfield toward the pad. A cadre of men folded out of the vehicles with exacting precision and crossed the field.

"I want as many guns on this site as possible. Get me at least four gunships. Fourteen men, full assault gear. This is the guy who took out ECHO in Philly." Lepus buckled himself into the jump seat as he barked orders, and removed a folded MP5 from beneath the kit under the seat. With a whirling motion of his hand, he told the pilot to wind it up.

"We have control of all facilities? You guys have nailed that shit down, right? I want intel on everyone in and out of the area, and sat support. If a mouse farts in that cabin, I want it on tape. And I want it now."

The NRO DELTA man threw him a salute and barked orders.

The copter spun up to full power in seven seconds, but only the vibration indicated it. Implacably silent, the Black Hawk slowly rolled up into the air, drawing away from the field. Lepus shucked the action on the submachine gun. Then he found himself watching his hand with dumb wonder.

He couldn't tell if the tremor he saw there was elation, fear, or simply the Black Hawk's silent mechanics working countless times a second, shaking his body like a tuning fork.

He didn't care.

Either way—although he couldn't identify what—he finally felt something.

Last Dance

Camp finds it: Rutgers University, New Brunswick, New Jersey. 40.48 N/74.46 W latitude/longitude: Approximately 200 miles from Mount Weather, Virginia: Saturday, February 10, 2001, 1:01 A.M. EST.

WHEN HE WAS SNATCHED, the weapon had gone off just once before it was shaken from his grasp, a hollow boom in the darkened parking lot. The gun skittered off beneath a car, leaving a trail of twisting smoke behind it. Despite fifty years of marksmanship, he had not seen or heard his assailants, at least not clearly, and the shot was wild, nothing more than the accidental contraction of an arthritic hand.

He knew he would never see that gun again, and dimly wished it well. Everything past that was a soupy blackness, his head fading into a humming dark, feeling as if it was stuffed with novocaine-soaked cotton.

When he rose from it, his body was a chorus of pain, but still far enough back in his mind to indicate he had not fully shaken the drugs. He was aware of what was going on. He was in the back of a van which was in motion. The windows were secured with plates, but a dim light crept in from the base of the door.

Who had him? Lepus, of course. He had not been as careful as he could have been, but the exertion necessary for caution was just beyond him now. In the minutes he had spent with Lepus, it had taken everything within him to keep from wheezing, shaking and sweating. Even sitting still and looking alert required an effort that was terrible in its scope. He felt like he was being hollowed out, a resource that once spent was never coming back. It was a feeling of being emptied.

Now, he would have one last chance. Lepus would gloat. Lepus would preen. Lepus would get up close with him. Lepus' guts would drop on his shoes before anyone realized what was happening. Then Camp could die, content with that one last annoying wrinkle ironed out.

Young people thought so little of his generation. They had saved the world from fascism and communism, and still they were underestimated. Why search him thoroughly? His gun was gone. He was an old man. What harm could he be?

Camp slid his numb hand down his leg, curling with a distant thrumming pain until his pulse was slamming in his temples. Sweat erupted all over his body. Just as it seemed he could not push any further, his hands found it. He pulled the buck knife from his sock. It was an old thing, wood and brass and big. With the weight in his hand, Camp relaxed and lay on the base of the van, bouncing and wheezing with his heart racing in his ears. For a long time his heart kept the thready, sickly-fast beat, but then, as his breath was caught and he tried to focus, it began to slow. He was cool in the dark of the van, looking up at a grooved white ceiling.

He brought he knife up before his eyes and worked it with his thumb. A four-inch blade, dull with oil, flicked out and glittered in the dark.

Camp smiled. One last dance.

He refolded it, palmed the blade and gathered his energies, what little of them were left.

THE DOORS OPENED TO a blue-white light. It was early morning, and Camp realized he had lost himself in the dark there for ten or more hours. He felt better, calmer, centered. Hands were on him now, and he opened his eyes. These people were professionals, there was no use pretending. The buck knife was tucked halfway up his right sleeve, held in place by his hand, and would drop into his palm with a slight movement of the wrist.

Camp was lifted like a sack of dried branches and placed lightly on his feet on wet pavement. Two hands remained on him as he steadied himself. Men in blue coveralls with mirror shades and blank faces flanked him. As his eyes adjusted, the world bled in, a wall of new bricks filling his view—another parking lot, somewhere. Too public for an execution. He could hear people milling about nearby. Cars. A bus stop. He could see it. Off to the left forty or fifty yards. A highway and rolling green and red dirt, a dozen students. Very public.

For a moment, Camp was confused. Interrogation? Torture? A grey door on the back of the building banged open. Another man in similar coveralls held the door.

Forrest James stepped out, his face unreadable. Camp felt only one second of regret before he dropped the knife into his palm. With a hand signal from James, the two men next to Camp snapped salutes and stepped away. A perimeter was taken up around them by the men in blue coveralls.

Camp had very little time. As James stepped towards him, Camp folded his leg, in mock collapse. It was a little more than that; if this bluff didn't work, it was likely he would smash to the ground, breaking God knows what in the process. It didn't fail. James' eyes lit, and he leapt forward crossing the space with a speed Camp's body remembered but could no longer execute.

In the cup of Camp's palm, the buck knife's blade slid from its oiled groove in an arc with easy grace.

James hooked an arm beneath Camp's armpit and held the old man to him, lifting his fragile weight. Camp and Forrest were eye to eye, with James hunched to keep Camp from collapsing. Camp hooked a wasted arm around James' neck. It locked there.

James felt it then. A thick knife tip pressed to his torso, hard enough to puncture skin. A hairsbreadth harder and it would pop into James' torso, spewing filth after it. A bad death, fever and infection and rot. The worst death. A traitor's death.

"Don't move," Camp said.

Already, their actions were noticed. Camp couldn't look away from James but he sensed movement.

"Stand down," James said quietly.

They stood like that, two wrestlers locked in place, for a few seconds.

"Joe, you've got this wrong," James stated with a frank plainness that resonated. Joe could hear his heart singing in his ears. There was uncomfortable shuffling going on the parking lot, but Camp didn't look away. He was searching James' eyes.

"I've taken control of MAJESTIC. I need your help," James said. There was no lie there.

"Kidnap me—" Camp wheezed.

"What could I do Joe? I couldn't invite you."

The two swayed for several moments.

"Swear it, swear it on Stephanie," Joe said, his voice lost in gasping breaths.

"I swear it."

Joe sat down hard, his face covered in sweat, heart racing, the knife clattered to the ground. It really wasn't a choice; his body wobbled beneath him, his head swam. An anonymous foot swept into his blurred view and kicked the knife away. God help him if he had miscalculated, God help the world.

A huge calloused hand appeared in his view. James' hand. Joe looked at it for a moment, and then reaching up, grabbed it as well as he could. He was pulled to his feet with ease, and stood there, legs still trembling.

"Come on. You need to see something," James said, and turned back towards the door.

Camp followed slowly. As he passed the men who stood guard, he thought he sensed a new respect there, a recognition that he had been once as they were now, even if time had taken most of him away.

"Sir," the last man said as he entered the door.

The man saluted.

HE READ WITH A speed that was disturbing. Lifting and turning pages as if they were composed of stiff tissue paper, calloused, blunt fingers stacking the pages like cordwood as he consumed them. James stood by, watching.

Finally, Camp placed the last page of the MAJESTIC report on the table. He put a hand to his mouth and coughed.

"Bostick found it," James said. "He spilled the minute he knew Kroft, Ross and Lepus were gone."

The room was nondescript. A foam-tiled ceiling, dull dun rubber tiles on the floor, a fold-out plastic faux wood table, three chairs. A student center, cleared and secured by MAJESTIC. The lights buzzed above them in an insect-like drone.

Camp squatted in a chair and considered the papers on the desk. The Passive Brain State Monitor and Display looked very bad indeed. The disappearances, Bostick's briefing. It looked very much like Lumsden had transcended the limits of the world, and going through had brought something back with him. This explained the dead boy, the attack in Pennsylvania and Poe's report.

To Camp it was another version of the same old story: the temptation of power from beyond, the consumption of everything human, the death of all involved. It was nothing new. The weapon was new, that was all. An electronic shortcut to the other side. People had been doing this for eons. It required commitment, it required skill, it required knowledge. Most failed. Until now. This device guaranteed transcendence. This device was a machine for making madmen fueled by the infinite, a machine for making a supernatural cancer, bent on destroying the order that held the world together.

"We need to destroy this. All of this. All data on the machine, every copy of the machine, anyone who ever used one," Camp said.

"Scanning the campus for magnetic anomalies, we found the device, hidden. It's sealed behind a wall. In fact, a whole portion of the building is sealed off—perfectly. The job is seamless right down to the maps and plans for the building. There's a heat source in there with it. It looks like a person."

"And?"

"We knocked down one outside wall. Inside there's a symbol on all the walls surrounding the room in the hidden section of the building."

James slid a photo across. Camp had wondered at it briefly as he sat to read. A photo, turned down so what it was could not be seen, a small IR date burned in the back of it.

It was a color photograph of a stone wall. A zig-zag symbol was slagged in fire there. What looked like Chinese characters. Camp had seen it once in a Chinese scroll that was written before Alexander the Great was born.

"It's a ward. Chinese. It means 'closure' or 'cessation'," Camp said.

"What do we do?"

"You know what we do. We go in."

IT WAS EASIER THAN expected.

When they arrived in the hallway, the men were frantically taking readings with book-sized devices, staring with a flat disbelief at the wall. The symbol was still there, but now the wall was split by a door. The door was plain, grey—similar to any number of the fire doors in the building.

"Sir, the door—appeared. Do you want—"

"No," Camp said.

James shook his head at the BLUE FLY team.

"Set up a perimeter outside. Nothing in, nothing out," James barked.

The men immediately folded up shop and exited.

Camp stepped up to the door and dropped his hand on it. The handle was warm to the touch. James stepped forward with him, thought of stopping him, and then held his ground.

Camp swung the door open.

Inside, Bob Lumsden sat in a school chair, the sort of uncomfortable wooden chair which creaks and groans as you struggle to find comfort. He glanced up at James and Camp as they stepped forward, wiping hair from his eyes with the ease of someone once human.

There was something else in the room. The implication of power so far beyond any that humanity understood that James found himself shaking. The being in the chair glanced at them, through them; it held them in its mind and made them real. The world spun because of this being. No, that wasn't right, it spun *unless* this being thought otherwise.

"Come in," he said, "I've been waiting for you." His voice was plain.

Camp never hesitated. He held his head up and walked into the room.

After a moment, Forrest James, a man who had almost died more times than he could clearly recall, followed. It took more nerve than he could have imagined to cross the threshold.

Δ

"When you find out there is no God—when you find there's something else—it takes some time to get used to."

Lumsden spoke in a quiet voice. It was wholly human, filled with emotion and fear and longing. James realized he was having trouble keeping up. What was said a moment before was gone. Like the words on a page of a book read too fast, they faded into a humming white, an emptiness of thought.

"I understand what has to happen now, to stop the end from coming," Lumsden considered his hands. Normal hands. Palms up, resting on his knees.

"How? How do we stop it?" Camp replied.

"Wait—" James said, and when Lumsden turned to face him, the words died in his throat. James had interrupted the two men as they quietly discussed the fate of the world. The universe.

"Do—how can we . . . trust . . . him," James finished, speaking only to Camp, trying not to think about the being in the chair across from them.

"That's all we can do," Camp said, finally and turned back to face Lumsden.

Lumsden held a hand out, and Camp took it.

Then they were gone, leaving Forrest James standing in an empty white room next to an old wooden chair. The absence of the machine, Camp and Lumsden was instant, and without any special effects. James considered the silence for a moment, his mouth open, and just before he lost his composure he clasped one huge hand to his mouth to stifle the noise there.

It was like a scream, the noise, but it died in a hiss between his fingers. He and Joe Camp had not been playing in the same game at all. Joe Camp was operating at a completely different level. It was only now, as his legs gave way, that James realized he had been the pretender after all. He had been a traitor, even if he himself didn't believe it until now.

James had believed himself a white knight. Someone who could protect America from the things that haunted the world.

James believed it.

Camp lived it.

It was dusk when Camp opened his eyes, but he knew where he was even before he saw it. The light which had filled the world had vanished, leaving behind only a dull yellow-red and the cold wind. The air smelled of water and ozone and and burning leaves.

Camp stood on the shore of a lake. The edges of the lake were tinged with ice, but it broke into chunks not too far out, replaced by black, still water. Trees surrounded the lake, blue-green firs rapidly dwindling to black as the color bled from the sky.

"How do I stop it?" Lumsden asked behind him.

Camp turned to find Lumsden standing twenty-five feet away in the burned-out ruins of a cabin. It was little more than a spray of cinder blocks and charred wood now. A single huge ceiling beam split the middle of the lot, overgrown with a rich, green moss swollen with frozen water. This place had been beautiful once. Now it was a gap in the earth, a sore. Something about it, something beyond the fact that it was burned to the ground, felt wrong. There was something here. Reality ran thin here. He had felt it before. Lumsden stood with his back to Camp, glancing down into the rooms under the ruins. The concrete bunker beneath it, where Reggie had made his last stand.

"That's the question I should have asked at the start," Lumsden said, quietly.

Camp glanced across the lake at his own cabin, and was for a moment overcome with the urge to walk there, to go there and to go to sleep in his own bed. To escape. To die there, alone.

Instead, he turned and walked towards Lumsden.

"Instead, I just . . . did things. You're here because you can undo what I have done. I started this. You can end it."

"Why me?"

Lumsden looked up.

"I don't make the rules. I thought I did. But I don't. When you move through, you imagine you are omnipotent. You think there can be nothing more powerful, but you're wrong. There are other things. Other reasons. Other gods. Power on varying levels that mix and change and move at the will of some force at the center of everything."

Lumsden smiled.

"You'll have to excuse me. It's difficult to describe. There's a . . . music that makes . . . everything. Certain places, certain people are—peaks in that music. Important. You are one of those people. So is Adolf Lepus."

Camp stood still.

"Lepus?" The word sounded like a curse.

"Yes. You and Lepus. You have both been close to this force that spins at the center of everything. You have confronted such things before. He has witnessed such things. You've heard the music?"

"Yes. But why now?"

"Because this is when this is to happen. Like any musician, I can hear the crescendo coming."

Camp placed his squat hand on his forehead. He brought it back covered in sweat.

"Can't you stop it? Can't you make something to stop this?" Camp finally said.

"No, no. You don't *create* things, you move things. That's how to stop it. You *hide* things. You don't destroy or create, you *borrow*. I was making things whole-cloth, I was removing things completely. This left—*gaps*. Things came though those gaps. You are familiar with them Joe, the *things*. You don't mind if I call you Joe?"

"No. I mean, yes, fine," Camp said.

"I'll tell you something, Joe. When I was on the other side, I saw everything. Every moment from the beginning to the end of the world. That's a lot of information to parse and it's only a blip. Even so, it's hard to focus. But here's what I know. My partner Garrity went through before I figured this out. Before I realized I could hide things instead of destroying them. He should be here soon. I will need you, Joe, when he comes. He's been looking for me. He thinks he is in control."

"Just tell me what we need to do," Camp said.

"This place—Fairfield cut a hole in the world, here. It's a place they can come, when they are called. You need to send us all, Garrity and myself, back to the beginning. You've done it before,'" Lumsden said.

Joe Camp turned to face his cabin and nodded.

"Let me show you how to use the machine."

Coordinate

Lepus approaches his quarry: 39.93 N/75.18 W latitude/longitude. Approximately 200 miles from the "Country Club": Monday, February 12, 2001, 4:55 P.M. EST.

THEY HAD REFUELED TWICE, landing the last time at a military outpost that looked like it had been abandoned in the face of an oncoming apocalypse. It hung on the jutting rock of a coastal inlet, an open tarmac landing pad, a few old tankers and a shack. Where it was, Lepus was not exactly certain. It was Air Force—that much he knew—but the men who occupied it didn't even ask where the Black Hawks were from. They just fell in and after briefly admiring the helicopters began to fuel them. Other gunships, attack copters, would rendezvous with the Black Hawks at 1730 just outside the target coordinates.

The Black Hawk pilots got out, compared maps, and smoked cigarettes. Good ol' boys who had flown dozens of missions of this sort, they looked amused with the level of manpower they were carting around. They considered the NRO DELTA troopers with certain, humorous disdain.

Four hours in, the chopper had set Lepus' back to aching. He stood out on the tarmac and considered the vast, rising face of a mountain to the west. Conifer trees rose uncontested from the base all the way to the summit. Lepus stood still, at the edge of a dirt road and chain-link fence, and tracked the path that wound to the top. This place seemed like the edge of the world.

Lepus' eyes found something in a spray of green and fixed there. Halfway up the summit, a split in the old growth revealed something, a man-made structure. Stone, maybe. It jutted from the ground like a huge grey tooth.

A low, pulsing drone shook him. It tracked up his spine and into his eyes, and for a moment he was certain he would see it when he turned. Instead, he found that the ground crew had produced an airjack and were doing something on one of the choppers. His men reacted to him, unconsciously reaching for weaponry. Lepus waved an impatient hand and the guns vanished.

He turned back to the vista and considered the trees in the growing dark. He turned back only when he heard the pre-flight checks being made. But even then, turning his eyes away from the forest seemed nearly impossible. Something was up there, in the dark, shaded from the sky. Something alive.

Something was waiting for him.

"Saddle up," he shouted, spinning a finger in the air. He hoped no one could see his fear.

AS THE COPTER SWUNG upwards, pulling away from the ground, Lepus' eyes tracked the forest below. As the Black Hawk banked, hovering improbably for a moment, in the dying rays of the day Lepus thought he could make out people walking on the trail up the mountain.

A thin chain of people, dressed in dun tones, walking up a trail in the forest in a picket line.

Towards something.

Then they were gone.

"Sir, eighteen minutes out from GIANT-KILLER," the pilot intoned over the headset. They were minutes away from meeting up with their gunship escort. They were also, if all checked out, minutes away from landing.

Lepus nodded. When he closed his eyes and turned his mind inwards, instead of the black expanse he saw something he hadn't seen in years.

He saw a light.

The Last Trick

Garrity senses something: ∞

GARRITY PAUSED, OUTSIDE THE world, watching, turning reality over in its mind like a silver-white mote of a billion facets. In these facets it saw many things. Snake-like creatures drawn from the sea to build basalt cities a billion years before man. Creatures that transited through the uneven corridors of time with nothing more than a thought. Every thing which had struggled to survive in the face of the pointless game called physics, every creature which had perished wishing for a moment more of time—which was, to Garrity, as useless as the world.

Garrity swung its gaze outwards only once, and a nightmare vertigo swept its consciousness. It was not the limitless stars, nebulae and oceans of gas that it feared, but the gaps. Between tiny sections of the mote, things watched. The gaps breathed and moved and squirmed, and Garrity, not really wishing to admit it, turned to reconsider the world out of something like fear. Fear of that last unknown. Garrity was not ready.

When it turned back, a mote was centered in its mind. A clear image of Lumsden and the machine, the Glass. This was strange. In the mote, it could not divine Lumsden's intentions. All was clear except Lumsden, who, like Garrity, was beyond the everyday mundanity of the world. Lumsden could be seen only after Garrity learned to look for the gaps that Lumsden left in his wake. Lumsden was a shell, and the thing in it roiled and moved and spread itself out to bathe the world, as seen through its shell's senses, in a light-like creation. Lumsden was showing the Looking Glass to a man.

Glancing at this image, perfect in its detail, Garrity could see all. A man was there with Lumsden, looking into the machine. The machine stood in a house in the woods, a place that Garrity now knew in absolute detail. Lumsden spoke to the old man, a man named Joseph Camp. Joe Camp was in the service of the government, or a thing like the government. Joe Camp had seen many things in his limited life. So much that Garrity, now beyond it all, was impressed. Garrity rifled through the reality which established what Joe Camp was, the wake his matter cut through the four dimensions of the world.

It saw a young Camp in fatigues standing in a desert in Australia in 1943; screaming in a jungle in 1942, swinging a shotgun like a baseball bat, bug-bitten and sick; sending agents to their deaths in 1998 by remote control from a quiet office in the basement of the Library of Congress. Speaking with something not human in China in 1951. Shooting people, lying, reading, thinking. Garrity tracked the life of Joe Camp to its end—but unlike the vast number of lives Garrity had considered in their absolute detail, the life of Joe Camp did not reach the precipice where the consciousness left the form, folded in on itself and vanished like a card trick. Joe Camp's mind swung out in vastness, a blue-black wave that swept the world and then went outside. Farther and deeper into the gaps than any Garrity had seen before.

And there was music in this change. Music.

Lumsden would recruit others to his cause.

This would not do at all.

It was true, Garrity could cut off at any point the wake through space-time called Joe Camp. It could seize the stream of particles that had the mind called Joe Camp stamped on them at any point in their history. Garrity could track the atoms, the fragments of energy which made the atoms, back to their eruption from the sun. It could scatter them, it could collect them, it could stamp them out of reality.

It could do all of these things and more.

But Joe Camp seemed capable of moving beyond.

Camp alone among them seemed poised to move into the gaps that watched the world from the edges of it all. He alone seemed to understand the last trick. The one beyond the Looking Glass, the one beyond the world and reality.

In an existence where every question was answered and every thought was reality—all except one—above all, Garrity wanted to understand this last trick.

Do You Want to See?

Alphonse throws down: Fairfield Pond, Fairfield, Vermont. 39.93 N/75.18 W latitude/longitude. Monday, February 12, 2001, 5:10 P.M. EST.

WHEN GARRITY APPEARED, IT already knew Camp had gone through the machine. Lumsden's wake had vanished from its vision on the far side, and when Garrity arrived at the cabin it was shaken to feel something like fear. Only Camp was here. It could see only Camp's wake in the world. Something else. Something was wrong. The feeling would not leave its mind, which hovered around its body like a perfect haze. It had imagined its arrival as an angry god—instead it felt weak, impotent. Not just frightened, but something worse: uncertain. Camp had done something which had made its sight from the other side vanish, change, distort and fade. Something unnatural.

Despite the change that Garrity could sense, Joe Camp looked the same. The same ruined body that had been shot, wracked with disease and fatigue and the slow play of death. Garrity knew every change in that body down the years it had tumbled through space, every shift, every failure, every pain. It was the same. Why had Camp not changed it? This more than anything bothered Garrity. Why would one suffer such indignity when a thought could change it? What could the motive be? What was the secret?

Camp turned, saw Garrity, smiled, and walked slowly down the long hallway. There was no fear or apprehension in Camp's demeanor. He seemed bored. Completely at ease.

Garrity was unprepared for this. Surely Lumsden had warned his pupil. Surely Camp knew him. Even if he could not see him, he could see the gaps he left in the world from the other side. He would know him. But perhaps Camp was different. His end was certainly different. Garrity had imagined a confrontation between Lumsden and himself, or with Camp. It had expected something, a conflagration of power. Instead, this.

At any point, Garrity imagined, it could stop Camp, though it had never used its powers on anything like Lumsden or Camp. What would happen? Perhaps that was part of the trick as well.

Garrity followed Camp down the hallway. He heard a shifting noise—the sound of wood pulled across bare concrete—and he turned the corner to find itself facing an empty stairwell. Below, in a dimly lit room, Garrity heard Camp speaking. The floor was concrete, with a piece of stained wood pulled over it at an angle.

"Do you want to see?" Camp asked from the basement.

"Yes," Garrity said, and followed.

It went down the stairs into the dark.

THE SIGIL WAS PAINTED on a piece of wood the size of a door—branded, really, with a soldering iron or something like it. The wood lay on the floor in the dark basement just beyond the last step, and when Garrity stepped on to it, it knew it was the end.

The symbol looked like a tree-branch, or an eye, or a pulse of flame, but then Garrity could not focus on it. Too much was happening.

Garrity's mind raced as it found itself caught within the circle. The power which bled from the thing called Garrity doubled back at the lines of the circle and looped, growing in light and force, causing Garrity to grimace. Its face pulled back in the rush of compressed energy with no hope of release. Its powers, which tried to reach out and change the world, simply redoubled on it, smashing into it with a force it could not long endure.

It turned inward to find the portal to the other side, and found that too, was gone.

Garrity squinted and saw Joe Camp in the darkened corner of the room, through the lines of power which circled him, Camp was doing something in the corner. There was someone else there in the corner with him.

Joe Camp erased the chalk lines from the floor, removing the elder sign from the feet of Lumsden, releasing it from a prison as real and perfect as had ever been made. Lumsden, freed, stepped past the ruined symbol towards Garrity, exploding in Garrity's sight like a sudden flare lighting in the room. Lumsden had been here the whole time.

Lumsden stopped, nodded to Camp and turned back towards Garrity, helpless in the light.

"I'll show you the last secret," Lumsden said quietly, he raised his left hand, and stepped into the sigil with Garrity.

"The last secret is that in the end, everyone dies."

Lumsden held a long, clean butcher knife.

The Edge of Infinity

Lepus sees: The Target Site. --.-- N/--.-- W latitude/longitude. Approximately 91 miles from [REDACTED]: Monday, February 12, 2001, 6:22 P.M. EST/The Temple of the Moon, Cambodia, Wednesday, February 12, 1969, 12:32 A.M./∞

TWO SWEEPS OF THE area by gunships had revealed only one heat target. Lepus sat in the jump seat with his gear ready as they orbited the site. Beneath them the world was drawn in blues and blacks. Otherwise it was empty wilderness and low, rolling mountains.

No lights were on in the house.

Lepus flipped down the IR rig and considered the world that floated below him in a shivering fluorescent green. IR spotlights traced arcs to and from the house. A mechanical gate to a dirt road; a track that swept past a fresh-looking cabin—little more than two gable roofs and four rooms dropped on the edge of a vast, dark lake. Nothing. Mundane.

Still, something stirred in his memory about it.

The GIANT-KILLER gunships reported a single human heat target in the basement. Intel indicated there were an unknown number of rooms underground. No plans for the site could be found. The vast network of machines and men waited on Lepus' orders. Lepus had considered dropping a few Hellfires down the chimney, but the idea—which had once seemed mighty fine—no longer seemed to make sense. Every time his mouth opened to order the airstrike on the house, something stilled it.

"Okay, take us in," Lepus spoke over the com, and felt his stomach lift and flip as the Black Hawk swung in to an open patch of ground to the south of the cabin.

He didn't need to look around to know there was carefully masked confusion on the faces of the NRO DELTA agents.

The Black Hawk touched down with a jolt but with little sound. Buckles were let loose as his two teams swung out in picket lines, goggles flipped down, guns clutched in firing positions, crouched, securing the landing zone. They swept forward implacably, like a rippling wave. Soon they would overspill the yard and take positions on the building.

Lepus, despite his fear, leapt out of the seat and pushed through the line, grandstanding. He marched forward with his MP5 slung, feigning fearlessness.

Despite his false bravado, when he found the front door ajar something moved in him. It was the feeling of routine. Of repetition. The feeling of tediousness as one sets to a task he has done a million times before.

He pushed the door open.

A long, narrow, tall hallway hung with timber rafters led to a open doorway. From this doorway a thin, pale blue light lit the night.

"Hold positions," Lepus said numbly over his radio, but he wasn't certain why. His men tensed, prepared for an attack.

Only his training told him his men were baffled as Lepus struggled with his gear, but it didn't matter anymore.

He placed the MP5 carefully on the cement stoop and slowly drew out his pistol.

It was the way it was supposed to be.

"Lepus, I called them," Joe Camp said. His voice was empty of emotion. All the melodrama was gone. Instead the voice was filled with the quiet certainty of a man looking at all he has left burning behind him.

Somehow, as if the world itself had been fast-forwarded, Lepus now stood in a stark basement, ripped open by a blue-white light. Joe Camp sprawled on an ancient, wooden chair. The center of the room above the battered piece of wood was engulfed with light. Two bodies were on the ground, torn and bloody and dead. Gutted. Ripped to pieces by inhuman forces. Someone had dragged the bodies towards the center of the room. Someone had drawn symbols with their blood. The room, the whole room was covered in markings and pentagrams and signs.

The blood glowed blue-black in the light. A light he knew. Had seen before, just as it had seen him.

The first time he had seen the light, it was on top of a temple in the jungles of Cambodia.

The light was a door. It was a hole in the world where something could slither in. Where something had slithered in, where something would slither in. It was the key and the gate. It was infinity.

"They've been waiting for you," Camp whispered. "For us."

Lepus' mouth was dry. His gun, forgotten in his hand, slipped and fell to the ground with a clank. Suddenly the basement seemed full of dead generations. Thousands of people long forgotten, some known to him, silently watching, screaming, crying, gouging their own eyes out, crawling, leaping, cavorting, dying. The invisible world that haunts the edges of physics spun through the air in a thousand different pictures. A million worlds, a billion moments, spun to this moment, fastened to this time by the light in the center of the room. A pivot in history, on which the entire reality of the universe spun.

The noise began.

Tipler was there, screaming about things from space. Waverly sat at a ghostly desk, considered a pistol and then blew his brains out in one, quick, practiced motion. Poe was there, crawling away from the Temple in 1969. Fairfield was there, grinning through stained dentures in 1994. Camp was there in 2001 trying to cover his yellow eyes. Lepus was there in 1969, 1996, 1999, 2001 and forever, watching.

This had all happened before. Was happening before. Was happening again.

This all *was*.

On the Temple of the Moon in 1969 the light ripped the night apart. At Vieques Island in 1999, Lepus watched the world spill away to the edge of infinity. On Fairfield Pond in 2001, Joe Camp turned away when he couldn't take it anymore and saw Reginald Fairfield, four years dead, sitting across from him, wounded and grinning a mad, clear grin, seeing him.

Lepus heard the music. A pulsing, wind-like whine shook and rattled every atom in his body. It spun his mind like a wheel, pulling all thought, all conception, all ideas of identity and consciousness down the gleaming, bone-white surface of everything. It poured over him. Through him.

Lepus realized, a moment before his mind was obliterated by the power he found there, that this was the reason for everything. That this music was everything.

Then he not only heard the music, he *was* the music. And he was gone. This moment was gone. The world around Fairfield Pond was gone. The Earth was gone. The solar system and reality to the furthest center of the ever-expanding infinity of the universe was gone.

All that remained at the center was the roiling, living, mass of something so huge, so vast, so worshipped and revered and primal that it could have no final name. Creatures circled the flames of its form and played the music, horrific angels circling the omnipotent fire, playing a dirge which made the world, the worlds, which made reality itself from moment to moment.

Lepus—although he was no longer Lepus—was there too. The powers that held eternity in their minds were sated, consuming what was once Adolph Lepus. And as the pipers danced and were once again restored to their pattern, the universe fell in behind them, down to its smallest detail, all plans of escape or destruction lost. The wheels which spun the engine of time found their spoke and began their slow turn.

The galaxies spun in their dance just as they had before.

Camp, in the moment before he was consumed by the forces he had fought his whole life, had one last thought—and that thought was: *Rest.*

Resolution

Undisclosed location. Friday, March 2, 2001, 11:32 A.M.

It had been years since Forrest James and Donald Poe had seen one another, and those years had not been kind. That was the first thing both of them noticed. James looked as if he had been subjected to years of emotionally and physically rigorous training, which had put an edge to every smooth surface of his body. Poe simply looked as if he had been running, non-stop, since they had last met. When their hands touched, the shake was light, as if they had no power left in them, or each was letting the other feel like he was in charge. In either case, there was something false about it.

A dozen unseen triggers tensed during that shake.

They both wore sunglasses, and neither could see the others' eyes. Both wore shoulder rigs under their coats, and both had the air of being backed up by unseen minions, stashed somewhere in the thousands of windows that overlooked their meeting place. Neither tried to hide the fact that they were wired and under surveillance—it was expected.

"How are we going to divvy this up?" James said.

"I've got the group," Poe said. "Joe dropped the dime before he went in. I have the files and the rerouter. We'll keep going."

"He was a brave bastard. The pond. The house. There was nothing left when we got there. No survivors. He took Lepus with him, wherever they went." James smiled, and found Poe grinning with him.

"Fuckin' A. He gave old Fairfield a run for the money, and I never thought I'd say that."

James looked at Poe closely. "Are you sure you don't want in? We can do some good."

Poe shook his head emphatically. "No way. You think you can

fight the good fight in there? Go for it. Maybe we can help. But I don't trust them, not any of them. I won't hand my people over to them. Joe knew what he was doing. We stay outside."

"So, you have my information?" James asked quietly.

"Yeah. I'll give you a ring if we need anything."

"So it's a truce."

"You guys handle your stuff, we'll watch for all the rest."

James nodded.

The two separated, and began to walk in opposite directions.

"Poe," James said, without turning.

"Yeah."

"Keep your head down."

"You too, man."

They both knew that if they were lucky, they would never see each other again.

Acknowledgements

THIS NOVEL WAS MADE possible by the fans of Delta Green who contributed to its Kickstarter.com fundraiser:

Tim Aldridge
Alise
Karsten Scheibye-Alsing
Jesper Anderson
Martin Andersson
Agent Jo
Iain Armstrong
Pako Ary
Temoore Baber
David "The Unnameable" Bagdan
Roland Bahr
Candice Bailey
Patrick Barrett
Nick Bate
Wolfgang Baur
Ben W Bell
René Beron
Tim Besko
Thomas Beuleke
Kristian A. Bjorkelo
Scott Blevins
Thomas Bockert
Marius Enge Bøe
Daniel Boisvert
J.F. Boivin

Jeffrey B Boles (Icarus)
Nate "Baron al-Mithal" Boothe
Mark "Najael" Bourcy
Michael Bowman
Ross Bowrage
Chad J. Bowser
Rob Boyle
David Bradley
Charlie Romeo Bravo
Julian Breen
Nick Brownlow
Christian Bull
A. N. Bundock
Steve Burnett
Chris Butler
Nick Butta
Aaron Buttery
Andrew Byers
Jeff Campbell
Sean Campbell
James Cannon
Martin Hunter Caplan
Jonathan Capps
Anand Capur
Peter Carlson
Matthew Carpenter

James Casey
George M. Casper
Robert Cawley
Ludovic Chabant
Pete Chenery
Brady T. Chin
Josh Clark
Matt Clay
Sylvain Clement
Jim Clunie
Robbie Cobett
Alison Colman
Joseph J. Connell
Simone Cooper
Brian Covey
Scott D. Craig
Andrew Craker
Colin Creitz
Brian Curley
Tom Cusworth
Thomas Dahmen
Neal Dalton
Ian Davidson
Andy C. Davis
Vincent Delaumenie
Steve Dempsey
Dave Desgagnes
Adam Di Gleria
Gus Diaz
Ben Dinsmore
Mark DiPasquale

Regis M. Donovan
Brian Dorion
Scott Dorward
John Dougan
Rodolphe Duhil
Darin DuMez
Dumon
Herman Duyker
Damien Dyon aka Cpt. Nathaniel Franks (MIA)
Nick Edwards
Stephen Egolf
Viktor Eikman
Tim Ellis
Mikael Engstrom
Dave Erickson
Escrivio
David "SuperDave" Farnell
Davide Ferrari
Ken Finlayson
Adam Flynn
Special Agent John Fosey
J. H. Frank
Frank Frey
Corey Fulton
Scott Gable
Egoitz Gago
Marshall T. Gatten
Sergio Silvio Herrera Gea
Patrick Gingrich
Felix Girke

Christopher Wayne Glazener
David Goffin
Allan Goodall
Duran Goodyear
Koen Goorickx
Samuel Graebner
Morgan W. Gray
Pete Griffith
Derek Grimm
Allan T. Grohe Jr.
Matthew Gromer
Ollie Gross
Trevor Blaze Guina
Chris Gunning
Judy Haber
Laurel Halbany
Ville Halonen
Josh Haney
Scott Haring
Dan Harms
G. Hartman
James Haughton
Morgan Hay
Martin Helsdon
Fred Hicks
Giles Hill
Maximilian Hoetzl
Jeremy S. Holley
Antti Horelli
Miranda Horner
Ross Howard

Jonathan Hsu
Richard Iorio II
Bert Isla
Frank T Jarome
Colin Jessup
Michael J. Johnson
Zachary Johnson
Jon Jones
Poh Tun Kai
Patrick Kapera
Leszek Karlik
Ralph Kelleners
Mike Kelley
James Kemp
Jussi Kenkkila
Reto M. Kiefer
Ben Kimball
Kit Kindred
Lyz King
Graham Kinniburgh
Michael Kleinbaum
James Knevitt
Johnny Ladevez
Ralf Lanwehr
Lars the Bridge Troll
Randall D. Larson
Ville Lavonius
Robert Lint
Roberto Linteau
Edward Lipsett
Henry Lopez

Tony Love
Mark Lowell
Lukulius
Bryce A. Lynch
M Jason Mabry
Joan MacDonald
Chris Malone
The Man in Black
Davide Mana
David March
Come Martin
mbourgon
Matt M McElroy
Calum McDonald
Ben McFarland
Seana McGuinness
Badger McInnes
Shane Mclean
Peter McNeil
Peter McQuillan
Joseph McRoberts
Dana Matthew McVey (WarDragon)
Nick Meredith
Patrice Mermoud
Jason Mical
Marcin Miduch
Christopher Miles
Jordan "Millandson" Millward
Neal Milton
Adam Miramon

Gary "Sneezy the Squid" Mitchel
Rob Montanaro
Roger Moore
Dr Moose
Oliver Morris
Todd A. Morth
Aaron Mungillo
Ryan Muzzey
William Nichols
Keith Nielsen
Peter Nielsen
Kirsty Nixon
Andrew J Noble
Chris Nord
Benjamin Norest
Ethan Novak
John O'Connor
John O.
Carl-Niclas Odenbring
Julian Orr
Dave Owen
Randall "WiseWolf" Padilla
Robert J. Parker
Gregory "The Razer" Parsons
Reverance Pavane
Luke Pendo
Kristian Bach Petersen
John Petherick
Robert Pfaff
Rob Pinkerton

Matthew Plank
Tom Pleasant
Pookie
Dave Post
Frank Prassel
Cesar Bernal Prat
Graeme Price
psuedononymous
Donato "Agent Donald" Ranzato
Frédérik Rating
Nikki Reed
Philip Reed
Reza
Mark Richardson
Peter Risby
The Roach
Matt Roberts
Stewart Robertson
David Rodemaker
Rodrigo (WiNG)
Kevin Rolfe
Aaron Roudabush
Michael Ross
Steve Rubin
Peter Sahlin
Nick Sakkas
Matthew Sanderson
Fidel Santiago
Gerry Saracco
R. Hyrum Savage

Adam Savje
Jakob Schilling
Bjoern Schroeder
Thorsten Schubert
Brian Schumacher
Scorpion RPG
Robert Shankly
Ralph Shelton
David A. Shepherd
Ori Shifrin
Mark Shocklee
Michael Short
Alexander Siegelin
Sean Silva-Miramon
Jacob Skowronek
Matthew (nerdwit) Smith
Dave Sokolowski
SpacedOut
John C. G. Spainhour
Sphärenmeisters Spiele
Trevor Stamper
John R. Stanfield II
Richard Starr
Greg Stolze
Bryce Stoddart
stosser
Bill Stowers
Alex Strang
Isak Strom
Maurice Strubel
Matt Stuart

Paul Sudlow
C.A. Suleiman
Chris Sylvis
Laszlo Szidonya
Ray Tessmann
Jeffery Tillotson
Tomas Aleksander Tjomsland
Craig Tohill
Tim Toner
David Tormsen
Csaba Gábor Tóth
Michael Tresca
Gil Trevizo
Martin Tulloch
Bruce Turner
Twyllenimor
Prakarn Unachak
Justin Unrau
Janusz A. Urbanowicz
Erik Van Buren
Jake van der Weide
Aaron Vanek
Steven Vest
The Veterans of a Thousand Midnights
Franck Vidal
Judas von Uberschnell
Matthew Wasiak
Phil Ward
Joe Watkins
Jason M. Watson
Petri Wessman
Bradley Neil West
Jonathan L. Westmoreland
Sean Whittaker
Rob Wieland
Charles Wilkins
Benjamin K Williams
Jason Williams
Wayne Williams
Bodine Wilson
Matthew C H Winder
Doug Winter
JoAnna Wioskowski
Stefan Wiskirchen
Dawid Wojcieszynski
Randell Wolff
Sid Wood
Justin Woodman
Graham Woodhouse
Steffon Worthington
Steven C. Zmuda

SPECIAL ADDITIONAL THANKS TO Martin Andersson, David A. Farnell, Davide Ferrari, Marshall Gatten, Kim Kuroda, Côme Martin, Mark Romaniw, Matt Stuart, Gil Trevizo, Phil Ward and Chris Womack for invaluable proofreading.

Printed in Great Britain
by Amazon